THE BILLIONAIRE'S CHRISTMAS PROPOSAL

A BILLIONAIRE FOR CHRISTMAS

VICTORIA JAMES

Entangled Publishing, LLC
2614 South Timberline Road
Suite 109
Fort Collins, CO 80525
Visit our website at www.entangledpublishing.com.

Indulgence is an imprint of Entangled Publishing, LLC.

Edited by Alethea Spiridon Hopson
Cover design by Heather Howland
Cover art from iStock

Manufactured in the United States of America

First Edition December 2015

To my readers,
Without all of you, this book wouldn't be possible. Because of your support I was given the opportunity to write this follow-up to my very first book, The Billionaire's Christmas Baby. *Both these books hold a very special place in my heart and I hope* The Billionaire's Christmas Proposal *will fill your heart with all the magic of the season.*
Wishing you and yours the very best holiday season.
Victoria

Chapter One

It was the worst day of her life.

Okay, so maybe not *the* worst. Maybe the second-worst day…no…well, it was definitely the worst day *this* month. Allison Barrington squinted at what remained of her apartment building, her eyes burning from the smoke. The orange blaze of the fire had mostly died down to an eerie gray smoke. It was still dark despite it being morning, but the red glare from the fire trucks and ambulances lit the sky, and the rush of emergency personnel buzzed around them.

"What a freaking disaster." No truer words had ever been spoken. Said words were uttered by her eternally sarcastic teenaged sister and roommate.

She turned to look at Danielle. "At least no one was hurt," she said, pleased that she could actually muster up something positive to say. It was all they had left, really. She glanced down at her dog, Captain Hook, who was currently peeing beside a lamppost.

"Hook," she said, giving his leash a gentle, but authoritative, pull. He looked up at her, his one eye locking onto hers before obediently ambling over. The eye patch on the other side had a smudge of soot on it. Deciding she needed to act confident and reassuring, she put her arm around her sister's shoulder.

"It's going to be okay, Dani."

"You say that about everything. This is not going to be okay. We have no apartment, no clothes, and seriously"—she paused to give Allison a once-over—"you are in desperate need of something else to wear. If this entire situation weren't so disastrous, I'd be humiliated for you. I mean, really Allie, flannel reindeer jammies and that ratty U of T sweater? Ugh. And that coat? At least button it up."

Allison didn't need to look down at herself to know what she looked like. But it was eight o'clock in the morning, and she hadn't been planning on standing outside in the crowded street while wearing it. She looked over at her sister, noting she was already decked out for the day. "Why are you dressed? The fire alarm went off at three a.m."

Her sister blushed slightly. "I was just—"

"Sneaking in, even though you promised me you'd be home by ten?"

Their conversation was interrupted as two young police officers walked toward them. "What a missed opportunity this is for you," Dani whispered in her ear. "Men in uniform everywhere, and you're standing here looking like a troll with a degenerate dog."

Captain Hook lifted his leg close to Dani. You couldn't ask for more loyalty than that.

"Gross!" she yelled, backing up a few steps. "So what are we going to do? Where are we going to stay?"

That was the million dollar question. She hadn't bothered getting renter's insurance, which meant everything would have to be replaced at her own expense. And yeah, she didn't have anything of huge value, and she wasn't on the brink of broke, so she could slowly replace things—key word being *slow*.

After a quick chat with the police and providing them with her contact info, she looked over at her younger sister.

"So now what? I'm not going back to Mom's."

No, of course they couldn't go there. Their mother was a train wreck, and they'd probably end up giving her money instead of the other way around. When she'd taken Dani out of there a few years ago, she'd promised her she wouldn't ever have to go back.

"What about the shelter?"

Allison shook her head. "We can't go there. They're beyond capacity, and now that they've been told they have to close…no." In the last decade of being on her own, she had learned how to survive. She'd built up her own life, gotten her dream job, and found friends she considered closer than most family. But since learning the shelter she worked at was being forced to close because of some big corporation wanting to use the property for its real estate value, it seemed she couldn't quite shake off the feeling of being tired. Tired of the fight, of the constant uphill battle she was facing. She never regretted for a second that she'd brought her sister to live with her, but it was another mouth to feed, more responsibility. And now this; everything in the world she had worked so hard for had gone up in smoke. Literally.

"Hello? Allie? Now what? I'm freezing."

Now what? She buttoned up her coat, knowing where they'd go. Maybe she'd known the minute it had happened. Maybe she'd been dying to call him the second she'd managed to get them out into safety. Maybe she'd wanted to hear his voice, reassuring her. He was the one person they could go to, and he'd take them in without question. The only problem was she didn't want to be indebted to him, or anyone. She also knew she could rely on no one but herself. She had learned that lesson at a young age, and being the optimist she prided herself on being, she could say it had given her backbone. Really, if she only relied on herself, then no one could disappoint her. She had no expectations of anyone, except herself. This theory/policy of hers did complicate relationships, because if you were used to always taking charge and never needed anything from anyone, well, the relationships became very one-sided.

Nevertheless, this was one of those times she was going to have to reach out, but it wouldn't be for long, and of course if he said no then she'd come up with Plan B. *Always have a Plan B, Allie.* Now they'd go to Ethan because…Ethan was Ethan. Ethan Dane was the guy she'd been trying to keep at a distance ever since her best friend and his best friend had gotten married. Their relationship was purely platonic only because she insisted it remain that way. She was either a saint for being able to resist a man like Ethan, or she was an idiot.

She looked down at her ensemble and cringed. Well, she had no choice; she needed to see him. "Let's go," she said to Dani and started walking away from the commotion outside the building.

"Uh, hello?" Dani said, catching up to her. The sidewalks were slushy, and the farther they went from the building, the quieter it became. Luckily, she'd been able to snatch her purse before evacuating the apartment. "It's like eight o'clock in the morning; where are we going? A hotel?"

Allison gave Hook's leash a little tug when he started lingering near a fire hydrant. This was not the morning for fire hydrant loitering. "No, we're going to see Ethan."

"Ethan? *Yes!* It's so great you have loaded friends."

"We're not going to overstay or take advantage. Just a couple of nights until we can get a new place."

"Perfect, then we can go to Hannah and Jackson's."

"No, they're at the cabin until New Year's."

"There's a bigger problem we need to address—you're

about to walk into your hot, rich friend's condo looking like that."

"It doesn't matter what I look like." Though she did cringe at the thought of Ethan seeing her looking like a bag lady…or troll. "Besides, Ethan's not at home now anyway."

"Where is he? And why are we walking?"

"He's at work, I'm sure—"

"At this time of the morning?"

"Most people work for their money, Dani." Ethan may have come from a very privileged family, but she knew how hard he and Jackson Pierce—his business partner and best friend—worked. It was one of the traits she admired about him…among others. Not that it mattered. Different worlds, different problems. And despite her turning him down three times, they had managed to maintain a friendship. They would be completely wrong for each other.

They turned the corner and made their way into the financial district, and Ethan's building loomed in the distance. It was dark and cloudy; the snow on the ground was now mostly brown slush. The sidewalks were full, most people dressed in suits and coats, rushing to work. Dani plowed through the revolving door at the entrance, and Allison couldn't help but gasp at the image of herself in the mirrored foyer. Her sister had been right. She looked like a hideous little troll. Bag lady would have been a step up. She avoided eye contact with people in the elevator and kept her head low.

They rode the elevator to the top floor, and she refused to look at herself in the mirrors again. Instead, she listened to the sound of her sister texting and held on to Hook's leash tightly as he attempted to make friends with the women in designer clothes. Judging by their expressions, no one had any sympathy for the dirty, one-eyed dog or herself. Her sister was at the opposite end of the elevator, clearly pretending she didn't know them. She nudged Dani out of the elevator when the doors opened, and the three of them walked past the almost empty reception area. The soft glow of a light at the end of the corridor made relief seep through her, until the sound of soft voices grew louder as they walked toward Ethan's office. They slowed and looked at each other.

"Sounds like a woman," her sister whispered.

She wasn't surprised. And she shouldn't be disappointed. Disappointment implied feelings other than friendship. She had none of those. None. She looked down at her clothes and tried not to weep like a baby. They peeked through the glass wall of his office. Allison ignored the tiny little flip her stomach did at the sight of Ethan. The man could wear a suit like nobody else. He was tall and built in a way that made it very obvious he didn't spend all his time sitting behind his desk. Ethan came from a long line of old money, and he carried himself with the confidence and dignity of a man who had grown up among society's elite but was also capable of striking out on his own.

When she'd first met Ethan—at their best friends' wedding—she'd been charmed, floored, and, well, smitten. And smitten was not a word that was part of her regular vocabulary, but it applied in this circumstance. He'd made it very clear he was interested, and she'd made it very clear she was not. He intimidated her. Not to mention the fact that Ethan hadn't had a serious relationship in…um, ever. She wasn't interested in being just another one of the women he slept with. So, difficult as it was to ignore the man's charms, she was determined. Even when he looked at her with those warm, whiskey-colored eyes and his mouth that always seemed to have a secret smile just for her. Nope.

So in the meantime they had become good friends. They saw each other frequently because of Hannah and Jackson and the fact that they were godparents to their first child, Emily.

Her sister nudged her, not taking her eyes off the window. "Who's Lawyer Barbie?"

Allison followed her sister's gaze. Lawyer Barbie indeed. What and who Ethan did in his personal or professional life didn't matter to her, or shouldn't matter to her.

"Actually, she might not be a lawyer. Maybe she's this hot model he's dating who likes to wear business suits that show off long, killer legs—"

"Stop talking." Her gaze moved past the woman, who was sitting in an unnatural pose on the corner of his desk. She did have killer legs, but Ethan wasn't noticing her—in that way at least. His gorgeous head was downturned, looking at something in a file.

"Maybe we should wait till she leaves," Allison whispered to Dani.

"Agreed. I feel even worse for you now. In fact, you're lucky I'm standing here with you so I can vouch for you in case security calls the insane asylum or whatever to drag—"

"Thanks. That's just what I needed to hear," Allison said. "Let's slowly walk back."

Hook suddenly started barking at his reflection with a fury, the high-pitched sound echoing in the silent office. Allison sucked in a breath as she made eye contact with Ethan. Mortification anchored her crappy rubber boots to the marble floor, and only the scattered bits of remaining pride kept her from weeping.

"Nice job, Hook," Dani muttered.

Allison wasn't paying her perpetually smart-mouthed sister any attention because instead of Ethan staring at her in horror, the man jumped out of his chair and bounded out of the room as though he were running to rescue his beloved... someone. But it was *her* he was running to, which made her heart swell and her throat constrict because the look in Ethan's eyes made her forget that she looked like an escaped

Christmas-loving sociopath. He made her feel like—

"What the hell happened to you, Allie?" The harshness in his deep voice was softened by the worry in his light brown eyes. His large hands gripped her upper arms and warmth seeped into her cold body.

"I, uh, I'm…" Her voice sounded hoarse, and she realized her throat was clogged with something akin to emotion… tears of some sort, because someone actually cared about her. Not someone—

"What's wrong with your voice?" he asked, frowning.

"I…um—"

Dani sidled up next to him. "Smoke inhalation. She almost died. Firemen had to carry her out of—"

"Jeezus, Allie." Ethan wrapped her up in his arms, and the last thing she saw was her sister's smug face before the rest of the world was covered by Ethan. His chest was hard, the arms that wrapped around her were strong and comforting, and the man smelled like heaven.

"Oh, you know this person, Ethan? I was about to call building security," the woman said, standing in the doorway.

Dani scoffed and stood at attention. "She's his slightly disheveled, but otherwise very hot, friend—"

Allison broke free from Ethan's embrace, feeling cold again. "Dani—"

Her sister shrugged and leaned against the wall again.

"Why the hell didn't you call me? How did you get here?" Ethan ignored Dani and the woman and ushered her into his office. She didn't bother looking at Lawyer Barbie as she walked past her—the woman's huff was adequate proof of her thoughts.

"Sit," Ethan said, shoving her gently into his chair. "Now tell me what happened."

He was leaning against his desk, fine lines around an undeniably beautiful mouth.

She glanced over at the woman currently sending her a death glare from across Ethan's sprawling office and crossed her arms. She was suddenly self-conscious. "I don't really want to get into all this," she whispered.

Ethan frowned and then turned around. "Nadia, thanks. You can finish your presentation at the meeting this afternoon."

Her sister then proceeded to usher the other woman out the door, shutting it a little too loudly to be polite. She flopped herself down on Ethan's couch, completely oblivious to her slush-filled clothes on the pristine leather. Satisfied she wasn't listening when Dani pulled out her phone and began texting, she looked up at Ethan.

"Well, what happened?" he asked.

"Our apartment building blew up!" Dani said before she could answer.

Ethan's tanned face went a few shades paler than the snow outside.

Allison turned in her chair to glare at her sister. "Stop eavesdropping."

She turned back to Ethan and tried to concentrate. She needed a coffee. "She's completely overdramatizing. There was a small fire in the building, and we had to get out—"

"Smoke everywhere, they had to put an oxygen mask on Allie's face."

He ran his hands through his hair. "Jeezus—"

"Stop talking, Dani." She continued to stare at Ethan, mesmerized by the look on his face. "It really isn't a big deal. No one was injured. I just...all our stuff is gone. We have nothing right now."

"None of that matters," he said in a voice that sounded thick with concern for...her. This caring, serious, protective side of Ethan was disconcerting. Flirty playboy she could easily dismiss. Big, protective, serious Ethan was a whole heck of a different ballgame.

"I wouldn't have come here except I didn't know where else to go. Hannah and Jackson aren't around, and I can't impose on the shelter," she whispered. He didn't know about her unreliable mother, and admitting that he was the only person in a city of millions that she could turn to was, again, disconcerting.

A look flashed through his eyes, but was gone before she could mull over its meaning. "You did the right thing. You and Dani can stay at my place."

"We'll need clothes and food."

Allie shook her head, embarrassed by her sister's big, teenaged mouth. "Just until—"

"Whatever. I've got more than enough room."

"I don't want to impose or intrude on your life. We'll be gone in a few days, I promise."

"Seriously, Allie, you're welcome in my home for as long as it takes."

The shiver that ran through her then was totally caused by the fact that she had walked through the freezing cold outside, not at all dressed for winter. Of course. It had nothing to do with the way Ethan said, in that warm, rich-as-a-cup-of-dark-hot-chocolate voice, that she was welcome in his home.

Danielle suddenly appeared at his side. "Great, then let's get the hell out of here."

"I come with a lot of baggage," she said with a wan smile, her gaze locking onto his, onto whatever it was he was communicating with that look. She couldn't turn away.

Captain Hook decided that would be the perfect moment to pee on Ethan's marble floor.

Chapter Two

"Oh this place will do just fine, Ethan. Just fine." Dani patted him on the arm and walked through the foyer, making herself at home.

He dropped his keys in the silver bowl on the hallway table and turned to the woman who always seemed to be on his mind. He hated to think how close she'd come to getting hurt.

"You sure you're okay with this? Danielle can be very endearing, but most of the time she enjoys being a pain in the ass," she whispered, scrunching up her nose. Allie was the only woman who'd ever managed to consistently intrigue him and appeal to him on every level. After she'd turned him down—*three times*—he'd expected his attraction to her to go away. It hadn't. In some ways, it had only increased, because he'd gotten to know her even better. And she was everything he'd ever wanted. Allison was nothing like the women he knew, and because of that she had effectively ruined all other women for him.

"Are you sure it's okay for Hook to stay here?"

He looked down at the dog who was pretty much the size of an overgrown gerbil. Hook was looking up at him with that one eye. What could he say? "Of course."

"C'mere, Hook!" Danielle yelled. Hook ran off in the direction of her voice, his nails scraping against the marble entry tile until he gained traction.

She unbuttoned her god-awful raincoat, and he took it from her hands. He told himself he shouldn't be checking out a woman who'd just been in a fire and was now vulnerable, but he'd worry about what kind of a man that made him later. Right now a little admiration was fine. And he did admire. Allie came up to his shoulder, all curves and sweetness that he wanted to sink himself into. She was beautiful in a way that could be subtle or striking depending on what she was wearing, but she was always gorgeous. Even this morning, standing in his foyer with rubber boots up to her knees, reindeer pajamas, and a threadbare University of Toronto T-shirt. She sneezed three times in a row then blew her nose after fishing for a tissue in her coat pocket.

He had never wanted a woman more.

"Bless you," he said.

"Thanks, I think I caught a chill out there."

He frowned again, thinking about what she'd been through. "You shouldn't have walked all that way to my office. I would have picked you up."

She waved a hand and pulled off her boots. She was wearing red and green polka dot socks. "You're already doing more than enough. I know you need to get back to the office, and I need to get to work—"

"You can't go to work today. You should call in sick."

She pushed off a clump of wet hair from her forehead, and he resisted the urge to offer her a hot shower, preferably with him. "People need me. I can't bail."

"What about clothes?"

She groaned as her sister emerged at the top of the hallway. "I was thinking the same thing. Also, I don't think I should have to go to school today. I've been traumatized."

Ethan grinned at Dani's suddenly forlorn look. "I'll give you a credit card, Dani. Go buy some stuff for yourself and Allie while she showers and gets ready."

"Uh no," Allie said, shaking her head and putting up her hand to silence her sister. "We can't accept—"

"Sure we can." Dani sidled up next to him.

"No, we can't. Oh my God, Ethan, don't give her your card," Allie said, her voice rising to a screech when he handed her sister his Visa.

Dani grabbed it and stuffed it in her jeans after asking for his PIN. Her hand was on the doorknob, and she yanked the door open. Allie shut it before she could get out and then whipped around to look at Ethan. Her blue eyes narrowed. "You cannot give her access to this kind of money. We may never see her again."

"You're too funny. I know how to be responsible. I'll get the basics. Boring work clothes for you and some cool new stuff for me. I really do need to insist on taking a personal day."

"Buy only what we need to get by for the next week. Then if you are really wiped you can take the rest of the day off to relax here."

"Well, I think I might stop by school to get some homework assignments…and let everyone know what happened," she said, suddenly looking excited at the prospect of reliving her drama.

"Dani, I think I'm too tired to even argue."

She gave a little shrug and then held her hand out, palm open in his direction. "Can I have the keys to your Porsche?"

He choked out a laugh as Allie gasped. "Sorry, kid. Take a cab."

"Subway, Dani."

"I think I like Ethan's way of thinking." With that she was gone, and he was alone with a furious Allison and Hook, who happened to be attempting a jump on to his sofa. Sadly, it didn't look like it would happen anytime this century.

"Sometimes I wonder how we're even related." She pulled her hair off her face again and her wet shirt clung to her. He let his gaze wander for a split second, and he cursed himself for checking her out again. She was freezing, and he was ogling.

"Come on, I'll show you where everything is for a shower and you can get warmed up." She followed him down the empty hall toward the guest bedroom. "There's only one extra bedroom in here. I had the other made into a home gym. So you'll be sharing with Danielle." He stopped abruptly when he realized she wasn't following him. She was standing in the center of the room, staring out at the view.

"This is gorgeous, Ethan," she said. The breathlessness in her voice made him stop and appreciate what she was looking at. The Toronto skyline was something he'd seen for the last ten years. He woke to it, went to sleep to it, drank to it, but rarely did he take the time to stop and admire it, or anything really— other than Allie.

He stuffed his hands in his pockets and stared out with her. Snow was falling in a soft, slow pattern. It was a gray day. Not one he'd think twice about. Certainly nothing he'd stop and admire. She turned around after a minute, shot him a smile, and then walked toward him. "Sorry. I know you need to get back to work. Point me in the right direction and then you can get going."

He glanced at his watch. Yeah, he needed to get back— not that he wanted to. He had a meeting this morning with his brother. They weren't in business together and he didn't trust him, but Ethan couldn't say no. Even though he'd wanted nothing to do with the family business, he was still invested personally. He'd wanted to strike out on his own—and had, with Jackson—to prove that he could. From a young age he'd learned that in order to gain his father's respect he needed to prove himself. Prove that he was a survivor. They'd written him off years ago, but he was still here. He and his brother had an ongoing competition—started and encouraged basically from birth. He had lost repeatedly to his brother during one year of his life. He had vowed that would never happen again.

He nudged his chin in the right direction and led the way. He pointed toward the kitchen. "Help yourselves to anything." He paused while Allie slowed in the doorway, then he pointed down the hall that led to his office and gym. "The only place that's off-limits is my office." He realized that sounded a little *Fifty Shades* and continued. "I just don't want your sister messing things up in there."

Allie gave him a look that made him think she knew he wasn't being entirely honest, and she'd be right. But he had private things, and since he hadn't been expecting houseguests, he hadn't had the time to…rearrange some items. There were certain things about himself that he didn't share with anyone. There were parts of his past that only his family knew about, and even then he wished they didn't.

He opened the door to the immaculate spare room and en-suite. It would be the first time this place was ever used.

"Oh, this is gorgeous. It's like we're staying at a five-star hotel. I totally owe you for this, Ethan. I'm coming off a horrid week—"

"What happened? I mean, besides your building burning."

She rubbed her eyes. "Haven House is closing."

"What? They can't close a shelter."

Allie sat down on the edge of the bed. "Apparently they can. It's a mess. We haven't told anyone yet."

"Maybe there's something I can do."

Her eyes locked onto his, and his gut tightened at the light in her eyes. It was almost like admiration or hope. Either way he was screwed.

"I don't know what you'd be able to do. I don't have all the details, but I can get them and let you know. All I know is that the landlord is selling the building, and it's totally within his rights to do that. And what new buyer would want to leave it as a shelter? It's in a prime location, and we're guessing it would be rezoned for a condo. That's all we know. I hate to ask for anything, I mean in one day I've asked you for a place to live and now—"

"You've never asked me for anything." He was well aware of the fact that she was the only woman in his life who never asked for a thing. He knew her pride, her determination to make it on her own, and he admired her a hell of a lot for it. Allie didn't give a shit about material things and appearances like the people in his circles. Like his family. She cared about things beyond the superficial, and a part of him wanted in on that, on that bigger picture crap that went beyond what his acquaintances were absorbed with. He wanted in on Allie.

He took a step closer to her, noting the way the pulse at the base of her throat quickened, liking that it did. He would have liked even more to pull her into him, feel her, taste her, and then keep her safe, and hell if that wasn't a first for him.

"I should probably get into the shower and start my day. I don't want to keep you, either." She took a step back and stumbled on to the bed. He had to force his gaze off her. He could think of a few good ways to start the day, and for once none of them had to do with the office.

He adjusted his tie, the feeling that his life had just become a hell of a lot more complicated jostling him. Time to go. "I'll find out about the shelter. I'll do whatever I can to keep it open."

"If we win the bid, we plan on closing the shelter and putting up a condo."

Ethan schooled his features, not giving anything away, as he stared across his desk at his brother. "What shelter?"

His brother rolled his dull eyes. "Haven House or something like that."

Shit. He picked up his pen and twirled it through his fingers casually, resisting the urge to stab it repeatedly into his desk. He leaned back in his chair and tried to not think of the conversation he'd just had with Allie in which he promised to find a way to keep the shelter open. And here he was less than an hour later sitting in a meeting with his brother discussing the demolition of the shelter she poured her heart and soul into.

"Why would you close the shelter?" He knew it was a stupid question, but he was trying to get his brother to talk and reveal anything that might be useful to him.

Carson scowled. That scowl was probably the only similarity the two of them shared, passed down from a long line of scowling Dane men. "It's a prime piece of real estate. The landlord wants out. It would be the perfect corner for the condo project."

"Right. The city really needs another condo."

"I get you're not into real estate, but I think you must still have some business sense if you run *this* company. Okay, so you and Jason—"

"Jackson—"

"Whatever, you're tech guys. You won't know what or even how to come up with a real estate proposal, so you should probably bow out of this before you embarrass yourself. Since when have you cared about the family business?"

He didn't care about the Dane building empire, not one

bit—from a financial perspective. What he and Jackson had built was more than enough, but he did care about the family business on a very personal level. He'd never let on, but it was there, in his gut, in the back of his mind, always. He'd been pushed out, and that wasn't something that had ever sat well with him. He didn't like being dismissed by anyone.

Ethan leaned forward in his chair. "We were both at that miserable brunch last Sunday. You know Dad opened this up to the both of us."

"Which is a mockery. He set you up to fail. I'm sure Mom put him up to it—pity, probably."

Ethan smirked. "I think you're the one everyone pities, Car." He didn't get the full joy of seeing his brother's face go all red, as he was busy in his own thoughts about this disaster. While sitting at their parents' dining room table last Sunday, their father had presented them this "challenge." Both sons were invited to present a proposal for what to do with the new property acquisition. Whoever won had first dibs on the business when their father retired. The only complication was that Carson had just revealed that it was Allie's shelter that was the property in question. He'd have to sort that issue out later. Right now, he needed to concentrate on Carson and shaking his confidence. Their father was a manipulator, and this contest was a fine example of how his mind worked. It was a shitty thing to do to Carson, honestly. Carson had worked with their father from day one, while Ethan had gone out on his own. The company should rightfully go to Carson. He had a sneaking suspicion Carson was right and their mother felt that Ethan should at least be given a chance. Since they all saw the empire he and Jackson had created as inferior, they probably thought "poor" Ethan deserved a shot at the family biz.

"Dad opened this up to the both of us. May the best man win or something like that, right?"

His brother crossed his feet at the ankles and smirked. "Then this should be easy."

"Then again, I guess if Dad were truly confident in your abilities he wouldn't have set up this contest. I haven't had to work a day in my life for Dad. Never had to hear his criticism, kiss his ass, you know, all the fun stuff you do on a daily basis."

He had the perverse pleasure of seeing his brother's cocky grin falter slightly.

"Or maybe Dad is feeling badly for you, considering the time of year and everything," Carson said.

Ethan squeezed the leather armrests on his chair. Ethan had learned from a young age to never let his father or brother see an ounce of weakness from him. He forced his muscles to remain relaxed, and he stretched his arms above his head and linked his fingers behind his neck, not breaking his brother's stare. "This time of year means nothing to me. It hasn't in a long time," he said, lying through his damn teeth. He'd rather spend the day with Dani and discuss fashion over admitting that this time of year did mean shitloads to him, that this time of year haunted him from the beginning of November until December. That this time of year reminded him of how weak he really was. But they had never had that kind of relationship, so he wasn't going to admit a damn thing to his brother.

His brother shrugged. "Sure. Well, let the best brother win, I guess."

"But we don't even own this land yet."

"No, but we'll outbid everyone. We'll get it. Proposal needs to be ready for December twenty-first. Drawings, everything. I'm not sure you even have the means to access that kind of—"

"I have friends in real estate."

"Really? I thought your only friend was Jason-from-nowhere-Pierce."

"Jackson." Ethan flexed his hands into a fist, knowing his

brother was trying to get him riled. Nothing like the Dane snobbery to make an appearance. He and Carson came from a long line of money and had attended only private schools with the country's elite. Outsiders were noticed. He'd never given a rat's ass about that kind of thing, but then again, he'd been exposed to a different side of life than his brother ever had. Maybe that had been the only good thing that had come of it. "I have other friends." The problem wasn't finding a company to do this for him. The problem was doing this at all. Not only would it be bad enough to stand by and do nothing while his family destroyed Allie's shelter, actually being the one to design the condo project was an entirely new level of asshole, even for him.

"Like who?"

How easily he fell into this competition with his brother. "Hayden Brooks." He watched with smug satisfaction as his brother tried to hide his displeasure.

"I wasn't aware you were friends."

"Went to school together. We keep in touch."

"Well, who knows if this would even interest him, being out in Vancouver."

"His company builds anywhere, and I also happen to know that he's in the province at the moment doing some business in a small town not that far from here. Still Harbor."

"What the hell kind of business would he be doing there?"

Ethan shrugged. He wasn't comfortable discussing his friends' personal lives with his brother. You never knew how Carson could turn it around and use it as ammo. "Personal. Speaking of, how's your wife?"

His brother squirmed in his seat, his cheeks growing red. Ethan knew full well they were getting divorced.

"She's fine."

"What's this, wife number three or four? That must be making quite the dent in your finances."

"As lovely as this was, it's time for me to go. I'm meeting Dad for lunch." His brother rose. Ethan remained seated. He ignored the silly pang of whatever it was that stabbed him in the chest. He knew his brother and father were close. Hell, they worked together every day. It shouldn't matter that they never invited him to the club. He wouldn't want to go anyway.

Besides, right now he'd rather be thinking about Allie. In his home, for days on end. He'd rather think about her in his shower, and about how she'd sought him out in a city of millions. She'd come to him for help, which meant that although she'd been avoiding each and every pass he made, she felt something for him.

His brother paused at the door and turned around to face him. Great. His brother loved delivering jabbing one-liners before he departed, like he'd watched one too many daytime soap operas. "Well, whoever Dad picks for this will inherit the family business. I only hope nothing happens to you between now and then…you know, considering it's November."

Nothing like his family to kick him when he was down. Ethan clamped down hard on his back teeth, a string of curses wanting to flow out of his mouth like hot lava. Instead, he held on to them, giving his brother a smile. "Don't worry, nothing's going to happen to me. Watching you self-implode will keep me around. Merry Christmas, Carson." His brother gave him a smirk and walked out.

Ethan stood as soon as the door was shut, and he cursed the entire way to the liquor cabinet. His brother usually got under his skin, but today was a whole new level. The competition. The mention of the time of year and his health. But the worst was what this was going to do to Allie.

He had to tell her that he was going to be one of the guys responsible for closing the shelter.

Chapter Three

Allie hung up the phone, relieved she'd managed to contact everyone she needed to. If her sister would hurry and return from her shopping expedition, then she could get dressed and head out to the shelter. She was determined to salvage a little of the day.

The front door opened and seconds later her sister barged into the room carrying what had to be dozens of bags. "Oh my God, it was the best shopping trip *evah*," she screamed, dumping everything, including herself, onto the bed.

Allison tried to quell the urge to yell and the looming panic as she spotted all the designer names on the bags. She shut her eyes and tried deep breathing, but it didn't work, especially when she reopened her eyes and saw her sister pawing the front of a leather Coach purse. She slowly rose. "Dani, you do realize that is going back, right?"

Danielle scowled at her. "Excuse me? Uh, no. Where's your gratitude? This purse is yours. I bought it for you. It's large enough for you to put all your work—"

"We can't afford—"

"I know, which is why it's *so* great that Ethan *can*."

"I have to repay him, Dani. We didn't win the lottery. It's a loan."

Her sister rolled her eyes and pulled out a pair of UGG boots. Allison shut her eyes and tried counting to ten. None of these useless techniques worked.

"Allie, your problem is that you don't know luck when it slaps you in the face. Ethan doesn't need or want you to pay him back. He's loaded. So why don't you show a little gratitude because I spent the whole morning giving you a much-needed wardrobe makeover. I bought stuff for work, stuff for play." She held up a Victoria's Secret bag and wriggled her eyebrows.

The thought of her sixteen-year-old sister picking out underwear for her was alarming. She didn't know what the bigger issue here was—the money they now owed Ethan, or a wardrobe picked out by a teenager. She sat on the edge of the bed and tried not to cry. Sometimes it was painful being the only adult. She was her big sister, but she felt more like Dani's mom. It made their relationship tricky.

"You probably spent two months' salary."

Dani paused in her frenzied unpacking, holding a scarf limply in her hand. "Seriously? That's how little you make?"

Allison groaned and covered her face. What was the point? She'd work out some repayment plan with Ethan later. Right now she needed to get dressed. She had people that depended on her, and the crisis here was over. Her sister had clothes, food, and a roof over her head. Time to move on with the day. "Okay, what did you buy for work clothes?"

Her sister smiled with smug satisfaction and pulled out a pair of dark skinny jeans, a pale blue V-neck sweater, and the UGG boots. "Wait, there's more," she said. Allison didn't breathe. A silver bracelet and necklace followed, then a gorgeous, pale blue push-up bra and underwear.

"Please tell me you bought some sports bras?"

Her sister scoffed. "Puh-lease. You need underwire. It should be mandatory for anyone over twenty-five. I'm aiding in anti-sagging."

Allison snatched up the clothes and quickly started dressing. "I don't have time to argue with you. I need to make an appearance at work. I already called your school and told them—"

"Wriggle your hips and then yank them up," Dani said as she watched her sad struggle with the jeans. She needed to make more of an effort at the gym once she figured out where they were going to live and how she was going to pay Ethan back. And how she was going to save the shelter. Right. So, never.

Dani pulled out a plush terry cloth robe. "I'm going to take a shower in that gorgeous spa bathroom. Then a little pampering."

"I need to be out of here in ten minutes, so I'm saying bye now. I'll see you tonight. Ethan left you a key on the front table, but don't be home late. I'll help you organize all your school stuff after dinner."

"Oh, dinner…I wonder what we're having for dinner. Do you think Ethan has a personal chef?"

Allison opened her mouth, but she didn't even know what to say. "Do you have cash?"

Dani shrugged. "No, but I don't need it. I'll bring this with me to school." She held up Ethan's card and flashed it around.

Allison almost had a heart attack. "Excuse me? No, you're not taking that to school. I will give you whatever cash I have in my wallet. Hand over the card."

Dani pouted.

Allison shoved out her hand. "Now. Buy your lunches for the rest of the week and pick up something for dinner on the way home tonight. I don't want to bug Ethan, and I won't be home to make food."

Danielle pulled out the Visa and slapped it in her hand. "You need to learn—"

"You need to learn when to be quiet. Go shower. Have a good day."

Her sister stomped off, and Allison eyed the remaining clothes for the day. At least her sister had good taste. Minutes later she was slipping into the boots, and she could hear her sister singing in the shower.

She paused outside the bedroom door, patting Hook on the head and eyeing the hallway she knew led to Ethan's office, bedroom, and gym. The look that had passed across his face replayed in her mind. He'd looked closed off, suddenly unapproachable, and that was unusual for him. He'd always been very open. It was one of the things that attracted her to him—in a non-romantic way of course. She was reading way too much into this. Obviously, the man must have realized his pristine bachelor pad was about to be invaded by two women. He clearly just wanted to make sure he still had his own space. Yeah, they knew each other, but they didn't really *know* each other. She was going to have to get him some sort of thank you gift. Or help out around the house. Or something.

Half an hour later she was walking through the doors of the shelter, ready to deal with whatever came her way that afternoon. This place always felt more like a home than a homeless shelter for teens. It was open around the clock, and there were many times that Allie had stayed here overnight. As soon as teens walked in, it was the staff's priority to make them feel safe. Everyone was given clean clothes, toiletries, and a hot meal. There was a floor for boys and one for girls, and the entire building had a capacity to house almost one hundred youths. What they did here was integral. It was a known place, in a central location. No kid wanted to be on the street, and so many of them came from abuse and violence, this becoming their first truly safe home. Daily routines, set meal times, and chores were necessary in building a sense of safety and stability—something most of them needed desperately.

"Hey, Allie!" Denise, the group home manager and her good friend, called out. "You okay?"

Allison nodded, taking off her coat and hanging it by the hooks beside the front door. She walked across the tiled floor and joined her friend. "Yeah, what a day. We're staying at a... friend's place." Why did she pause at the word friend? That's what Ethan was. It must be her sister; she was messing with her head.

"Oh my God, I was so scared when I heard about the fire. What are you going to do?" Denise was currently finger-combing her long, curly hair into her trademark ponytail atop her head. Just seeing the familiar motion made Allison feel calmer for some reason. Maybe it was a sign that not everything had gone to hell.

"We're going to stay there until I can find us a new place." She walked around the front desk to the small coffee station. She could use a cup. Or an entire pot.

"Should I even ask if you had renter's insurance or anything?"

Allie winced. "I didn't have extra money for that." She dumped a bunch of milk into her coffee, stirring it slowly. "Bonehead move in retrospect, but between Dani and student loans, I couldn't justify it. I was so close to balancing everything and now I have to start over." She took a sip of coffee, hating to admit this aloud. She would never say anything in front of Dani, because she didn't want her sister to feel like a burden, and she'd never say anything to Hannah, because she knew her friend would force pity money on her. And Ethan... admitting this in front of him would be humiliating. Again, one of the things he'd never understand. She knew he'd grown up with money, lots of it. He would never get this. He was already doing enough.

"You'll manage. I'll see if there's an available apartment in my building. And whatever extras I have, I'll send your way when you're setting up."

Allie smiled at Denise. She had become a good friend since Allie moved to Toronto a few years ago. This entire place ran because of Denise. She put in long hours and was the rock behind it. "Thanks, I might have to take you up on that."

"Well, as long as you and Dani weren't hurt that's the main thing."

Allie nodded and looked around, making sure no one was within earshot. They absolutely didn't want word getting out to the youth that the shelter might be moving. This was the only place most of them could rely on, so the idea that it might be taken away from them could be devastating. "What are the odds? First the shelter, then my building? Any news about…?" Her voice trailed off purposefully, and she lifted her brows.

Denise shook her head. "No. Every time I pick up the phone I brace myself for some news, but so far I've got nothing."

Allie drummed her fingers on the wood surface. "I guess we're going to have to wait and see. And pray for a Christmas miracle."

"Speaking of which, I want to go forward with the tree trimming and decorating night next weekend. What do you think?"

Allie nodded. "Absolutely. We're not canceling anything."

"Perfect. I'll send out a memo to the staff and you and I can go over the finer details maybe tomorrow?"

"Sounds good. I'll plan to stay late tomorrow night and see about picking up some extra goodies to go with the hot chocolate."

"Perfect, sweetie. Call me if you need anything, okay?"

Allie nodded as Denise stood and began bundling up for the outdoors. "I still don't know why you even came in. The day is almost over."

"You know what it's like. I have appointments. I didn't want to cancel on anyone."

Her friend wrapped her red scarf around her neck twice so it covered her mouth, her hat tucked down low. "The world will go on without you for a day, you know, Allie."

Her words came out muffled, but Allie understood. She nodded and opened the door for her. Denise gave her a wave and walked out. Allie shut the door with a shiver and began her usual rounds of the house before settling into her small office on the main floor. This place had become like a second home to her, and the kids felt like an extension of her own family. She had even managed to get Dani in here on a regular basis to volunteer wherever extra help was needed. Sometimes they'd be short-staffed in the kitchen, or they needed extra help sorting the various donations that came in. It kept Dani focused and stopped her from feeling sorry for herself. Yeah, their mom had screwed up and both their fathers had been MIA since birth, but their lives could have been much worse.

Three hours later, Allie was finishing up with one of the house's newest teens and she was pleased with how their session had gone. They were standing in the hallway outside her office, close to the entryway. Max was sixteen and had come to live here a month ago. He hadn't really opened up to them much, but Allie felt like she was making progress.

He'd been living with his single mom who was an addict and verbally abusive, but she had only figured that out by reading between the lines. Max had lived on the street for about a month before coming into Haven House. He'd been cold, standoffish, starved, and beaten down, but he'd been given clean clothes, a shower, and a bed, and when she'd walked in the next morning to meet their newest teen, her heart had gone out to him. It was something that happened on a regular basis. She would always remember the way the kids looked that first day when they arrived, and most often it was completely different from when they were ready to go on their own again.

The shelter had a strict sobriety policy, so kids had to be clean in order to live here. Max thankfully had an aversion because of his mother. He was also extremely guarded, which was normal. They had to earn his trust. Routine, shelter, and daily meals went a long way in earning the trust of most of the teens.

"See ya," he said, flicking his chin in her direction.

Allie smiled at him. He never called her by name. He didn't call anyone by name, but she knew it would come, in time. Names were personal to some kids. Calling people by name meant a familiarity, and he obviously wasn't ready. "Have a good night, Max."

He shrugged, his gaze darting down the hall. "Okay. Uh, hey, I wanted to ask you something first."

"Sure. Do you want to go back in my office?"

He shook his head. "Uh, I was just wondering about Christmas. What happens? I mean, like, are you guys going to be working during the holidays? Do we have to find somewhere else…to go?"

Allie had perfected the serene look on her face during her first year of social work. She never wanted someone to see her surprised. She wanted everyone to feel like their questions weren't alarming or revealing—even when her heart was breaking. She knew exactly where Max was going with this, and the insecurity in his voice, in his stance, pulled at her. "Of course we're working. Haven House never closes. Ever." As she spoke the words, doubt crept into mind. How could she even say that considering the threat against the shelter? Well, she wasn't giving up. This place would always be here for them. It had to.

He nodded and took an awkward step back, but not before she caught the look of relief on his face. "Oh. Okay."

He started to walk away, so Allie quickly kept talking. "Christmas is the best time around here, you know. We put up a tree, decorations, there's a special Christmas Eve and Day menu. Presents." She smiled as she spoke even though he was looking down at his feet. She knew this was overwhelming for him, but she hoped by Christmas he'd start opening up a bit. It would be his first Christmas away from his mother. During their sessions, she knew he didn't want to speak about her. She knew it was normal for him to feel anger toward her, but it would also be quite normal for him to miss her or feel concern for her. Christmas was about family, and it was difficult for kids without one, which was why they went above and beyond during the holidays.

Max looked to the door as it opened. Ethan walked through looking like the cover model for GQ magazine. Even when he wasn't at work, success and power clung to him as beautifully as his tailored suits. A gust of snow swirled around him as he shut the door, and her heart fluttered. He brushed the snow off his hair and made eye contact with her from the across the hall, giving her a wave and a smile that could melt a thousand snowmen. He was holding a paper tray, two red cups inside.

"See ya," Max said, looking back and forth between them, and walked away.

"Bye, Max. I'll see you tomorrow."

He didn't turn around. She saw Ethan give him a nod as he passed by.

"Hey," she said, walking up to him. "What are you doing here?"

"Your sister texted me asking if I could pick up takeout."

Allie groaned, and he laughed. "I gave her money to get her own food." Knowing how her sister's mind worked, she'd probably thought she could save more money by tricking Ethan into paying for dinner.

"And then she told me you were working late and that you'd probably walk home. I, uh, didn't want you walking home after dark, so thought I'd pick you up."

Her heart swelled at the thoughtfulness. He was one of the good ones, she'd always known that. But the way he spoke, the warmth in his gaze and in his deep voice was enough to make her forget all the reasons she'd made up about why she couldn't be with Ethan. Not that he'd still want to. She'd come up with stupid excuses each time he'd asked her out. Now he was just being a decent guy. She'd be silly to be reading into it. "Well thanks…you didn't have to. I don't want us to start being a burden, and as for Dani—feel free to ignore her. Once you start answering her demands they'll only escalate."

He smiled warmly at her. Good lord, the man had the power to charm the socks off her just by smiling. "Well, I was also told that you like a late afternoon coffee." He handed her a red cup, and she admired the white snowflake design.

She accepted the cup, a warmth and tingle sweeping through her as her fingers brushed against his, which had nothing to do with the hot beverage. "Thank you, this smells so good."

"I figured since you drink so much of it you should have the good stuff. It's organic, single origin. Roasted locally."

"What flavor?"

He made a face that was both arrogant and adorable at the same time. "No flavors. Real coffee. Try it."

She took a sip and moaned, closing her eyes as the rich flavor hit her. "Sooooo good," she whispered. Ethan's garbled cough made her snap her eyes open to look at him, but he was busy sipping his own coffee. She forced a casual expression on her face, holding her cup a little closer. "So what do you think of Haven House?"

Ethan looked away for a moment, but not before she caught a flash of something in his eyes. Right. Of course this wouldn't look like anything much to someone like him.

"Never mind, silly question, right? I'm sure this looks like nothing special."

"It's special," he said. His voice almost sounded harsh and his gaze was intense on hers. "That kid you were talking to looked like he was only fifteen or sixteen."

She nodded. "Yeah, Max. He's one of the newer kids. Really nice, I can feel it. Sometimes I get a feeling about people, you know? Even if at first they're kind of rude or cold, I can sense who they are underneath."

He didn't say anything for a long moment, those brown eyes of his filled with a depth that made her want to know how much more there was to him.

"Is this your office?" He flicked his chin.

"What gave it away?"

"The Christmas tree, the empty coffee mugs, and the picture of Danielle on your desk. Also, you were standing right in front of the door."

She laughed, watching as his gaze wandered the room. She stood aside so he could walk in. "I guess it's a little different from yours, huh?"

He filled up the small space, hands in his pockets, gaze on hers. "I like it," he said in a low voice, the barest hint of a smile on his face. Her heart started to race, and she walked into the space with him. She was drawn to that expression in his eyes, the affection, or whatever it was that was reeling her in. "There's a lot you don't know about me, Allie. I think what you're doing here is incredible. I think you're gifted. I think you're practically a damn saint."

"I don't think you're supposed to swear and say saint in the same sentence," she said, babbling because somehow Ethan was now standing within an inch of her. The craziest thing was that she couldn't be sure who had approached whom. And right now she really didn't care, either. Also, his praise was a little too much to handle. Ethan smelled like the outdoors and a hint of some fresh, clean cologne. His hair was now mussed up and he looked delectably male and gorgeous up close.

"I gave up trying to impress the higher-ups a long time ago," he said in a way that seemed to hint at something. She couldn't pursue it, because her phone vibrated. The sound was jarring in her quiet office. She swallowed hard and forced herself to back up a step and glance at the phone.

"Ugh. It's my sister. She wants to know if you're coming home with dinner soon."

Ethan smiled, and all of a sudden it was like the moment was lost, her questions fading. Ethan's undivided attention was disconcerting in all the best ways. "You can tell her yes. I stopped and picked up food, too. I'm parked out front."

"Thanks, but seriously. You don't have to do all this." The noise from the dining room increased, and the sounds of chairs scraping against the floor signified dinner was starting. She was done for the day.

He shrugged. "It's not a big deal, Allie."

"Actually, it is. I also need to speak to you about some sort of repayment plan—" She stopped talking, because he sounded like he was choking.

He gave her the full-on, intense Ethan stare that robbed her of her voice. "You're not paying me a damn thing." His voice was low and filled with warmth…delicious, single-estate, dark-roast-organic-coffee warmth.

"You cannot give a teenager access to that kind of money," she whispered, moving closer to him so that no one would overhear. She made it a point of never talking about money or dressing too showy, which wasn't usually a problem. But even today she'd been self-conscious in her designer gear, at least it had been casual.

"Don't worry about it. Dani got everything you needed?"

Allie nodded. She found herself standing close to him as they walked to the front door. Every time she stood this close to Ethan he managed to evoke feelings of safety and excitement, both of which were foreign feelings for her. His cashmere coat clung to his broad shoulders, and his trademark blue tie peeked out from underneath. Everything about him exuded wealth and power. Things that should mean nothing to her, except they also symbolized how hard he worked and how talented he was to be able to build a company from nothing. She darted her gaze away from his face, which was looking far too appealing this close. His five o'clock shadow seemed to only highlight his strong, lean features, and framed a gorgeous mouth.

He placed the tray of coffee on the front desk. She reached for her coat, but Ethan had already intercepted and was holding it for her. She stepped into it and felt as though she were stepping inside a decadently warm bubble bath that was scented with Ethan. She tried not to sigh at her stupidity and picked up her new bag.

He held the door open. "Ready to go?"

She nodded. "Yeah, thanks. I'm wiped," she said, grabbing the tray before they stepped out into the cold night air. She hugged her coat closer and walked with him to his car. Somehow he'd managed to find parking on the perpetually packed street. Minutes later they were pulling away from the curb and she was feeling the intimacy of the small luxury car around her. Ethan shifted gears and drove through the city streets with a confidence that she added to her growing list of things she was impressed by.

"Did you manage to salvage your day after we ambushed you?" It felt odd to be sharing details of their day. They usually hung out in the company of Jackson and Hannah, not really on their own, and certainly not like this.

He nodded. "Yeah, how about you?" He pulled into his parking spot in the underground garage. He retrieved two bags from Whole Foods as well as his leather laptop bag and swung it over his shoulder.

"Yeah, I'm glad it's the weekend. I need to figure stuff out and sleep." Figure stuff out like where they were going to find an apartment, how much she had in savings, finding cheap furniture, and how the heck she was going to replace what they'd lost, all before Christmas. "This'll be my last free weekend probably until Christmas. Next weekend is the annual holiday decorating party."

They rode the elevator to the top, just the two of them. "Nice. So you get the entire place decorated?"

He held the door for her as they opened on to his floor. "We do. Tree, garlands, the works. It goes a long way toward making the kids who don't have a real home feel good. Christmas is all about family, and when you have none, or at least when you have none that you can rely on, it means even more. If there are kids who celebrate different holidays during the season we make sure we honor their traditions as well. These kids may put on a tough act, but they are heartbreakingly vulnerable. That's why this news about the shelter possibly closing is even more serious." They were standing outside his door, talking softly in the empty corridor. He was still holding the bags in his hands, but the look on his face stopped her from speaking. She didn't know what it was. He looked…upset maybe. "Oh my God, Ethan," she said, touching his arm. "I'm not saying all this to make you feel bad. I know you offered to help, but I totally didn't expect you to solve the problem or even think about it today."

He cleared his throat and looked away for a moment. "No, no, I…want to help. I just…yeah, today I couldn't get to it. But I want to help you, Allie."

The way he said her name was almost magical. Like he actually really, really cared. She waved her hand. "I know, I know, let's just enjoy the fact that it's the weekend. We already hijacked your home and now you're buying us dinner. Seriously."

"Do you need help next weekend? With the tree?"

He was a saint. What had she been thinking these last few years? Obviously she had judged the book by its cover, and she had been so wrong. This hot, beautiful, *compassionate* man was now even offering to give up his Saturday night for her. She forced a normal smile on her face, not the pathetically happy one that was inside. "We always need help, but you don't have to. It's Saturday night."

"No plans," he said, unlocking his door and holding it open. She walked through and again caught that whiff of whatever cologne he wore—it was something fresh like the ocean, not strong, just a hint. Hook came barreling toward them like a raging bull, and they both bent down to greet the dog.

"Then sure. We'd love that. I hate assembling the stupid tree."

His head was close to hers as Hook demanded more attention. "Assembling? No real tree?"

She tried to remember how to speak, but she wasn't prepared for Ethan this close up, offering his services. "Not in the budget. It's too much of a hassle, too."

"I'll get a tree."

"Oh my God, you guys, it's about time. I'm dying of starvation." Her sister appeared at the top of the hall and then marched forward, grabbed the bags, and groaned as she walked toward the kitchen. "Whole Foods, really? I was thinking more along the lines of McDonald's."

"I'd rather die, Dani," Ethan said dryly as he hung up his coat.

Dani was opening the takeout containers, making faces as she looked in each box and laid them out on the black marble counters.

"Dani, maybe you should say thanks."

Her sister rolled her eyes. She settled on a sandwich with a reluctant huff. "Thanks for the food. I know it must be hard when you're old to think of what young people might like to eat."

"Well, you might not get to be old if you eat garbage." His voice was laced with a smile, and Allie watched him. He dealt with her sister like she was amusing. He wasn't the least bit bothered.

"Wine?" Ethan asked, turning to her.

"Sure," Dani answered before she could.

"Not you," he said with a laugh.

"Yes, please. You may feel the need to drink on a regular basis now that my sister has moved in," Allie said. Ethan took out the wine glasses and poured while she took out dishes and forks.

"I'm going to my room," Dani said, almost out of the kitchen.

"You're not eating food in our room."

"It's fine. Cleaning lady comes in every morning at nine."

"This is the life," Dani whispered as she exited the room.

"Where do you want to sit?" Ethan asked as he helped himself to a sandwich and salad. Allie picked up the same for herself.

"I'm easy. Wherever."

He grinned. "Easy is hardly how I'd describe you." He led the way into the living room and she followed him, picking up her wineglass. Hook followed them, in the hopes he'd get handouts she was sure. They settled on the dark leather couch. Ethan had the fireplace going and only the dim glow of a table lamp lit the large space, but the city lights helped illuminate the rest of the apartment. Again that intimacy they'd never shared was back. Snow fell in swirling patterns outside the windows, and she felt as though they were in a protective, warm cocoon.

She took a sip of wine, and they ate in silence for a few moments. Everything was delicious. Things could have been very different tonight if he hadn't rescued them.

"I'd never been to Haven House. It's an impressive place."

She nodded. "It is. Almost one hundred kids right now, at capacity. It's a sad time of year for most of them, so we're busy trying to make it a special year even if they're on their own."

"Do they just walk in off the street?"

"Most of the time. It takes a lot for some of them. Many of these kids are so dejected, and depending how long they've been on the street, it can be really hard to reach them. But when you do—when they finally start to open up—it's like reaching a whole new person. And usually it's from that point that their life starts taking off. No one wants to be on the street, especially a teen. When we provide them with a bed that's their own, food, and showers, they learn to trust again. That's why I'm so afraid of this place shutting down, Ethan." She was horrified at the tears that seemed to appear out of nowhere in her eyes. She had no idea what Ethan was thinking, but his face went a few shades less than his usual tan.

He ran his hand over his jaw. "I, uh, I still need to see what I can do to help out."

She nodded. "I haven't said a word to the kids. We're not going to unless we have no choice. I don't want anyone freaking out at this point, and we have a few vulnerable teens at the moment."

He cleared his throat and put down his sandwich. "What

about moving the shelter to a different location?"

She shook her head. "Where? We're right downtown. There isn't another place that's large enough to support us, or at least without having to make significant renovations, and we don't have the time or money for that. And just the thought of such a big change, of uprooting them, is awful. People know where we are. The shelter has been in that location for fifty years, since it opened. Kids know where to find us. To move…"

He was staring at her, his mouth downturned. He looked as though he was really bothered by it. "But maybe if you move you can get a more modern facility, more amenities…"

"We'd lose a lot of kids not being in the downtown area. We don't need amenities. We need stability."

He didn't say anything for a moment. "I'll see what I can do."

She smiled. "I know you will. I appreciate it. Wow, you keep coming to my rescue. First a place to live, now the shelter."

He ducked his head, a muscle in his jaw moving. "Allie," he said, his voice thick with what sounded like regret. He was obviously humble, which was news to her, because she'd always thought Ethan kind of full of himself in a charming kind of way. Evidently she had a lot to learn. His phone vibrated on the couch between them, and he cursed softly as he looked at the number. Not that she was being nosy or anything, but the name on the display said Hayden Brooks. She had no idea who that was.

He looked up at her before answering. "It's a call I need to take, I'm sorry," he said, rising. She sat on the couch by herself as Ethan walked out of the room and down the hall that led to his office.

Chapter Four

Ethan took a long drink of his freshly-made green smoothie. He leaned against the kitchen counter and mentally ran through the plan he'd come up with to keep Allie happy and beat his brother in the little challenge their father had come up with. It was brilliant.

Sure, it may not be exactly what Allie had in mind, but in the end he knew she wouldn't find fault. He just needed to convince her — once he had some details and plans to present to her. With his plan everyone would win, except Carson, which was perfect. Except two minutes later he found himself thinking about the woman sleeping in his spare bedroom and feeling slightly guilty about deciding not to try and save her shelter. Every day Allie went on and on about how nice he was. If she only knew the truth. Since that couldn't happen he'd spent the week trying to avoid her. Now that his plan was fully formed, he could go back to normal.

"Dude, it's six o'clock in the morning. Must I be awoken like this?"

Ethan almost choked in surprise. Dani was standing in

the doorway, hands perched on her hips, her usual scowl even scarier at this time of the morning. It was still dark out, and he'd finished a run on the treadmill and had prepared his daily green smoothie in the Vitamix. He was running half an hour late, but he had a full day ahead of him. Plenty of time to put some of the first parts of his "screw over Carson" plan into motion.

At least all this crap going on meant he wasn't constantly thinking about D-Day. It was next week, and he hated that day more than any other. But it would be fine. He'd get through it, he'd get good news, and then December could unfold nicely and he'd be allowed to indulge for the month. He just needed to get through the next few days unscathed, be at the top of his game, and not let an ounce of vulnerability show.

"Uh, hello?"

Ethan glanced up from his smoothie to Dani. "Did I wake you?"

"You woke up the freaking building, I'm sure." She trudged into the kitchen, her bare feet flapping against the wood floor like a duck's flippers.

He took a sip of his drink, leaning against the counter. "I make this every morning. I've never woken either you or Allie."

"I have a lot on my mind. Must be stress."

"You're, like, twelve."

"I'm *sixteen*."

"Same thing."

That earned him a glower of the worst kind.

"Where's the coffee?"

"I didn't make any. I usually get it on my way to the office."

She groaned. "Listen, we need to get some caffeine going ASAP, before Allie gets up. She's a beast in the morning."

This time he did choke on his smoothie. He couldn't picture Allie anything but cheerful. She was always put together. Even after the fire in her building, the woman had managed a smile at his office. He put down his glass and pulled out a jar of ground coffee. Dani grumbled around, cupboards slamming and lots of huffing and puffing while he made the coffee.

"You really need to get some normal people food in this place." She swung open the fridge, made a face, and then shut it. "Too much protein, not enough carbs."

He finished the rest of his smoothie. "It's a shame this is the first morning our paths have crossed. I love being told how to eat by a sixteen year old." Dani didn't actually bother him. He kind of found her antics and theatrics amusing, like if he had a kid sister.

Allie walked into the room looking completely alien, almost like she'd been drop-shipped from a one-hundred-year coma into his kitchen. Her hair was all crazy, and she was rubbing her eyes. She had on a pink robe that gaped open, leaving him with the nicest view he'd ever started his day with. The pink tank or camisole was low cut and clung to delicious curves and a flat stomach. He heard a snarky noise and found Dani smirking at him. She saw him checking out her sister.

He cleared his throat. "Morning, Allie."

He thought he heard a garbled good morning back, but couldn't be sure. Dani verbally ambushed her sister about some school gossip and some party that she just "had to go to" that Allie had already said she couldn't attend. He poured a large mug of coffee for Allie, who was now sitting at the table with her head in her hands while Dani kept on talking.

"Here, sweetheart."

That got her attention. Allie jerked her head up and sent him a look of gratitude that made him wonder if he should have just brought her coffee all those times he'd asked her out.

"Anyone want a smoothie?"

Dani made a gagging motion. "I'd rather die, Ethan."

"Thanks, this is what I need," Allie said, getting up to grab milk from the fridge. Once she poured in a heap, she took a long sip and moaned. He wasn't going to get caught looking again, no matter how sexy her noises were or how good she looked with her eyes closed.

"Well, I'm outta here. Have a good day, ladies."

"You're going already?" Allie was looking at him. She appeared normal now, her hands wrapped around the mug of coffee.

"Yeah. Anything you need?"

She peered at him over the rim of her cup. "Do you have plans tonight?"

"Of course he does."

He shot Dani a look. "No plans…well, actually I have a dinner meeting but nothing after that."

"Allie, he's not going to want to help us."

He leaned against the counter and studied Allie. She looked beautiful without makeup. Not that she usually wore a lot, but seeing her like this made her seem younger, more vulnerable. "What do you need?"

"I have approximately one hundred gifts that need wrapping, and I was hoping to get it done by the time the tree goes up. But I know you're crazy busy, and you're already giving up Saturday night."

Dani leaned forward in her chair, looking back and forth between them. He pretended not to notice what she was implying. "He is? I haven't heard of this."

Allie ignored her, too. "But I'll make eggnog and bring home some stuff from the bakery." Like she needed any of that; he wouldn't have said no.

"I'm in."

"I'm out," Dani said, standing.

Allie frowned and pointed to the chair. "Sit down, you're

not out."

He walked to the door and then paused, remembering his meeting. "I'll be late, but I'll be here."

She nodded. "That's great. Thanks, Ethan."

"I need to discuss my weekend plans, people."

Allie winced. "You're sure you're still okay for Saturday? The Christmas tree lot?"

He grimaced. "I think we need to get out of the city and go to one of those…places that sells trees."

Allie's face lit up, and she even put her mug down on the table. "Really? I know a great farm."

"You're not taking him to Blueberry Hill."

Allie nodded.

He shrugged. "Whatever you want. Sold."

"So let me get this straight. Ethan is going to slap a live Christmas tree to the roof of his Porsche?"

"We'll take the Range Rover."

Dani sat up at attention. "I had no idea you had two vehicles…this gives me options."

Allie turned to her. "This information does not change your life at all."

"You really have trouble getting into the Christmas spirit," Dani said, slinking down in the chair.

"Anyway, see you tonight," Ethan said.

"Have a good day. Thanks for the coffee." He held her gaze for a moment, taking in her gorgeous smile. She was standing in his kitchen, like she belonged there, like she wished him a good day every day, except she wouldn't be looking at him that way if he didn't convince her that it wasn't important the shelter stay in its current location. Now that he had Allie in his house, the last thing he wanted was to lose her. He could have everything if he executed his plan properly.

Dani let out a scream. "Oh gross. Hook just puked on the rug!"

After she finished cleaning the rug, Allie made her way back to the kitchen. Dani was eating some kind of organic cereal from the box, flakes missing her mouth left and right and falling on the floor.

"Make sure you clean up after yourself," Allie said with a frown.

Dani rolled her eyes. "Ethan has a cleaning lady, Bertha or something. That's her job."

It was a wonder how her sister went from rags to riches with such obnoxious velocity. "Don't forget we're going to Mom's this morning."

Dani groaned and dropped her head onto the table, the cereal box falling and the contents spilling. "Why do you insist on torturing me?"

Allie closed her eyes and counted to ten. "It's Christmas. We're going to have a coffee, give her a Christmas present, and then leave."

"I'm not spending my day off from school hanging out with a woman who never had time for either of us, which is kind of ironic because I thought people who don't work have lots of time."

Allie finished off her coffee, not wanting to admit that everything her sister said was true. "She has issues."

"What did we get her?"

Allie paused. "A Dr. Phil book, a box of chocolates, and a gift card to Whole Foods."

Dani's head shot up. "You're freaking kidding me. Whole Foods? I think that's a bit of a waste, considering most of her grocery shopping is done at two a.m. at the 7-Eleven down the street. And a Dr. Phil book? She'll never read it."

Allie crossed her arms, trying not to get defensive. "I don't agree, and it's too late to have an opinion. I paid for all of it. I asked you for input—"

"I would have bought her a one-way ticket to hell."

Allie rinsed her mug in the sink before loading it into the dishwasher. "Which is precisely why I went shopping on my own."

"How can you be so okay with this? With her? She's a crappy mom."

Allie sighed and leaned against the counter. She focused her gaze on the dark cabinets, the richness of the wood in the modern kitchen. It was too early to be dealing with family problems. It seemed like her problems just increased instead of getting solved.

She still hadn't found a decent apartment for them. It seemed the landlord was still intent on selling the shelter, and she may have to face the fact that it was inevitable. Then on top of all of that, it was time to visit their mom, something she secretly dreaded. Going to visit her was always a disappointment and a reality check. Day-to-day she didn't think about their mother; she didn't resent her, she wasn't angry at her. But when they actually went to visit, all those buried feelings stewed inside until she was filled with this dark energy that dragged her back into an even darker place.

She glanced over at Dani, who looked as though she needed some reassurance. Time to act like the grown-up. "She's the only one we have, sweetie. I'm not subjecting you to living there, or going there for weekly visits. She's not a bad person, and she's had a hard life."

"So have you. So have I. We're normal."

Allie raised an eyebrow, and her sister actually blushed slightly.

"You know what I mean, Allie. She uses her bad past for an excuse. She acts like a kid, and she can never get it together. She puts her boyfriends ahead of us. She doesn't even love us."

Allie knew her sister's frustration. She knew it because she agreed with a lot of what she was saying. The only difference was that she had come to peace with it. There was also the fact that at one time her mother had made the right decision. But Dani had no idea about any of that. "Dani, you're young and you're pissed off at her, I get that. You haven't forgiven her, and it might take a while, but the sooner you let go of that anger toward her, the happier you'll be. And of course she loves us in her own way."

Her sister scoffed. "Did you read the Dr. Phil book?"

"All I know is that the more I was mad at Mom, the angrier I became in general. I didn't teach her a lesson by being angry. I just ended up hurting myself. We're not going to change her. The odds are not in our favor that she's going to wake up one morning and have an epiphany, try and turn her life around, and make it up to her girls. It's not going to happen. So we forgive. We don't forget, but we forgive. Move on with our lives. We have each other."

Dani glared at her for a moment and stomped out of the room.

"Go shower! And hurry, I have a bunch of stuff to do later," Allie said. She couldn't acknowledge the self-indulgent behavior.

The only response she received was the slamming of the bedroom door. She sat down at the table and dropped her head into her hands. Normally, dealing with Dani just required patience, but when it came to discussions about their mother it also required her to hold on to her emotions. She didn't know if she was giving the right advice. She didn't know if these yearly Christmas visits were doing more harm than good. Hell, she didn't know much at all. She looked like she had it all together. She was qualified to help teens, but sometimes she barely felt qualified to run her own life. What if she was screwing her sister up even more than their mother had?

She glanced at the clock, relieved that it was still early. She had a massive to-do list, and it was her day off. All she needed to do was get through the visit to their mother's house and then she would spend the evening with Ethan. Which she felt inexplicably giddy about, as though it were a date or something. Of course, it was not.

Two hours later they were standing in the smelly hallway of her mother's building. They had already decided the smell was a mix of pot and fish.

"I'm not knocking, you knock," Dani whispered.

"I'm holding coffee and presents, so if you want me to knock, you're holding all this stuff."

Her sister scowled, huffed and puffed, and then reluctantly knocked on their mother's apartment door. Their mother opened the door minutes later, as far as it could open considering the amount of junk, and squealed, pulling them both in for a group hug. "My girls," she yelled. Allie tried to keep the coffee from falling and refused to make eye contact with Dani, who was currently making gagging faces.

They followed their mother into the small kitchen, trying to weave in between boxes and garbage. "It's like we're visiting a future episode of Hoarders," Dani whispered.

"Shh and sit down," Allie said to Dani, who was standing in the doorway with more attitude than usual on these visits. Their mother was trying to clear the table from the assortment of magazines, lottery scratch cards, and dirty dishes. A few minutes later she sat down, and Dani reluctantly followed. Allie tried to concentrate on the smooth taste of her coffee, which was from the place Ethan had now gotten her hooked on, and not on the fact that their mother, whom she'd called the week before to arrange the visit, hadn't bothered cleaning up or getting out of her robe. It made her angry, not for herself, she was over that, but for Dani. She was already regretting forcing her to come here today.

Their mother was staring expectantly at the bag. Allie sighed and slid it forward, forcing a smile on her face. "Merry Christmas, Mom. It's from Dani and me."

Their mother smiled like a kid on a sugar high and plucked the red tissue paper from the bag and dug in. Her smile faltered as she read the title of the Dr. Phil book, but the gift card and chocolates were well received. "Whole Foods… sounds fancy."

"It's a little bit of a step up from the 7-Eleven," Dani said. Allie kicked her under the table, but their mother wasn't even following.

"Thank you so much, girls."

"It's all from Allie," Dani said, slinking back in her chair.

Her mother took a sip of coffee, not the least bit offended. "I wish I had better news for you girls, but this has been a really tight year for me."

"Here we go," Dani said, a little too loudly.

"And I wish I could have bought you presents."

Dani leaned forward. "Let me guess. You gave it all to your douchebag boyfriend, who spent it on the slots?"

Allie shook her head and shut her eyes for a moment, but not before seeing her mother's face crumple into tears.

"He should have won. And if we had won, I would have given you girls half of it. That's what I'd love to do for you—wait a second," her mother said, jumping up. She rifled through a kitchen drawer that couldn't fully close because it was filled with so much junk. She grabbed something and then spun around to face them, holding it behind her back. Allie groaned inwardly. "I do have something!" She marched over to Dani and placed a pack of Christmas M&Ms on the table in front of her.

Allie placed her elbows on the table and lowered her head into her hands, blocking out her mother's smiling face, and braced herself for the fallout.

"You have got to be kidding me," Dani said.

"You don't like them?"

Allie leaned forward and tried to get the conversation back on track so she didn't have to dwell on the fact that their mother had just attempted to pass off a forgotten pack of M&Ms as a carefully thought-out gift. "Mom, you know you don't have money to waste at the casino."

Her mother sniffled into a threadbare tissue and sat down. "Oh, I've learned my lesson, Allie."

Dani let out a choked squeal.

Her mother stuttered for a moment and then began speaking. "I know this must look bad, but things are really picking up for me. I have a job interview next week, and Bill does, too. And you know I hate to ask for anything, sweetie—"

"Really? You ask Allie for things all the time."

Allie braced herself for whatever was coming; she didn't even bother telling Dani to be quiet.

"I just need five hundred dollars to cover rent, and I promise to pay you back."

Allie shut her eyes for a moment, forcing the sound of her mother's voice into the back of her mind, along with the sound of Dani's chair sliding against the linoleum floor. Five hundred dollars. She wanted to yell at her, shake her. She said it like five hundred dollars was so easy for her to come by. She wanted to yell and say how dare she ask her for money when she was raising her daughter. She opened her eyes and stared at the gifts she'd bought for her. She slowly looked over at Dani and was sorry she'd dragged her here. It's not that she'd expected their mother to have made a major life change, but she'd hoped for…something. Something that might give Dani a little bit of peace.

It was time to go. She stood up. Her mother whispered her name, wrapping her hand around her wrist. "Allie remember, remember I helped you. I was there when you needed me most."

Allie paused, looking down. She hated this. She hated that Dani was watching so closely. She never should have brought her here. Allie squeezed her eyes shut for a moment, trying to not think of the event that her mother spoke of. There were so many things Dani didn't understand. She opened her eyes, not looking at her sister. "I, uh, I can give you a check," she whispered.

"What?" Dani yelled. "Mom, you know we were in a fire, right? Like, there's no extra money?"

Her mother was wringing her hands, her gaze darting around the room. She was looking for a bottle. "I know…and I'm really sorry I couldn't take you girls in."

"We wouldn't have come here anyway."

"Dani, wait for me by the door," Allie said, taking her checkbook from her purse.

"You're a weak, spineless coward, Allie! I can't believe you!"

Allie clenched her teeth, pausing as she stared in her bag. Her stomach rolled uncomfortably. She forced a deep breath. "Go to the door. Don't speak to me until we get back to Ethan's." Dani stomped off to the front door.

Her mother's hand grasped hers. "Thank you, Allie."

Allie stomach started rolling again, and she pried her hand away from her mother's. She didn't want to be touched. She took out her pen, wrote the check, and placed it on the table.

"Merry Christmas," Allie said, then walked out the door. She stood in the hallway for a moment. Dani was waiting in front of the stairwell. She tried her hardest to be the bigger person, the wiser person, because that's who she'd had to be her entire life. She walked toward her sister, wishing for someone to walk beside her, because she'd always walked alone. Right now it was like everything was falling apart, worse than ever, and she just didn't feel like trying to be cheerful or wise. She wanted to have her own meltdown. She hated that her mother still had that hold over her, that with just one reminder, she could bring Allie back to the most vulnerable time in her life.

Her sister's blue eyes locked onto hers, and Allie could tell she'd been crying. Her heart squeezed, and it seemed she was able to muster up that responsible person, because she put her arm around her and gave her a hug. "I know it sucks, Dani. But we have each other."

She expected her sister to hug her back, but Dani pulled out of her hug. "I can't believe you did that. I wanted to take those freaking M&Ms and—"

"Hey, I know."

"I am never coming here again. I'm never seeing her again."

Allie nodded slowly and reached out to touch her sister's arm. "It's okay."

Dani shrugged her off. "It's not okay, and I'm still pissed at you for being a doormat."

"Don't talk to me that way."

"Why, what are you going to do? Kick me out, not give me food? Fine, then do it."

Allie schooled her features, compartmentalizing her hurt, and used her professional skills, pretending Dani was one of her kids from work. She knew where this was coming from. When she had taken Dani out of their mother's care, it had been out of necessity. The promises her mother had made Allie had all been broken, and Allie'd had no choice but to pull her ten-year-old sister out. She knew Dani hadn't gotten over the feeling of abandonment. She also knew that Dani had no idea why she still felt indebted to their mother. "We're stuck together, kid."

"I'm done, Allie. I don't want to be stuck with you anymore. How can you be so tough and so stupid at the same time?"

Hurt slashed through her. Allie stared into her sister's eyes and tried not to cry. She saw the maturity there, years ahead of where she usually was. She owed it to her sister to tell her the secret she'd kept buried from her for so long. "I've been trying to protect you. I know you already despise Mom, and I just didn't want to make it worse."

Dani stood there, fiddling with the red scarf around her neck and watching her. "What are you talking about?"

Allie kept her voice low and tried to make it brief. "I gave her the money because I owe her."

"For what?"

"For choosing me." She looked down at her boots, wishing she could take back what she'd started. She never opened up to anyone, but maybe it was time. Maybe it was time Dani understood everything.

"Choosing you over what?"

"Over her boyfriend at the time. She took my word for something. She took my word over his," she whispered, trying to rein in her emotions, the memories, so that Dani would remain calm.

"What was it about?"

Allie looked over Dani's shoulder, concentrating on the glowing EXIT sign. "He, uh, started coming into my room at night."

Dani squeezed her eyes shut and covered her ears, shaking her head. "No, no, no, I can't deal with this. No."

And then she was gone. Allie watched her disappear down the empty stairwell, tears blurring her vision. She wouldn't go after her now. She could barely breathe. Just starting to speak had drained her of all the strength she had left. She had just spoken about something so dark from her past, and she was shutting down. She wanted to sit down and cry. For once, she needed someone around her to be stronger than her. She never should have said anything to Dani. She wasn't ready. She got that she needed to blow off steam, and she knew Dani had a good group of friends. So Dani would probably go to her best friend's house. And she…this wasn't something she could tell Ethan. How could he possibly understand this? She looked around the filthy hallway, the smells that were familiar now clinging to her clothes. No, Ethan would never be able to relate to any of this. Where she was, who she was, would never be enough for Ethan.

Chapter Five

Ethan straightened his tie as the elevator doors opened. He made his way down the corridor of the Dane Building Group, the familiarity of it roping him into thinking about all the times he'd been here as a kid, a teenager, an adult.

When he'd been little, he'd wanted to work here, alongside his father. He had always thought that was his destiny. His father would bring him into work and Ethan would listen attentively, fascinated by meetings and the way his father commanded authority. He loved how smart his father sounded. He wanted to be just like him. He had always been smarter than Carson, worked harder than Carson, and at one point in his life, his father had known that. He and his father had bonded. Until the day the doctors told them all just how weak Ethan was. That was the day he and his father had grown apart. That was the end of his trips to the office with his father. The end of being connected to his father and the beginning of Carson's rise to power.

For a while, Ethan had been too sick to care. He'd seen it happening, he'd sensed it happening. He felt like a toy that had been rejected for not being perfect anymore. Even when he'd recovered, things didn't go back to normal. Ethan had to work harder just to prove that he was capable of doing what he could before. But his father's faith had been lost, and so had his.

Little competitions began between him and Carson, their rivalry only growing. He knew Carson had been threatened by him, and there was no way Ethan would let him win. Despite all his accomplishments, his better grades, his extra-curricular achievements, none of it was good enough for their father anymore.

Ethan stopped outside the boardroom, his gaze wandering over the employees sitting at the long table. His father was at the head; Carson sat to his right. A long time ago, Ethan had imagined himself sitting there. Maybe this competition was his father's way of giving him his rightful place in the company. Maybe his father really did want him beside him now.

Ethan grabbed the door handle, his hand clenching the cool steel bar tightly. Too bad he wasn't doing any of this for that reason. He didn't want to sit beside his father anymore. Or any of them. He just needed to prove that he *could*.

"Mr. Dane," a voice called out.

He turned to see his father's secretary walking toward him.

"Don't worry, Rose. I'm going to see myself in."

Conversation petered out as he approached the head of the table where his father was sitting. The surprise and gleam of pride in his father's eyes should have filled him with satisfaction, but for some reason it didn't. Someone brought him one of the leather swivel chairs, and he sat down next to his father, opposite Carson. His brother's face was red and it looked like he was ready to break into a sweat, which was precisely the reaction he wanted. Ethan never came to these meetings. He knew Carson saw it as Ethan marking his territory. He liked to think of it as that and also enjoying being a shit-disturber, just as Carson had mercilessly done to him when they were younger.

"Hi, Dad," he said as he sat down. He turned to everyone at the table, some of the faces familiar. "Good morning, everyone."

He settled into his chair and gave Carson a smirk.

His father stood and gestured to him. "For those of you who don't know, this is my talented son, Ethan. He's decided to surprise us and listen in to today's meeting. Hopefully one day we can convince him to join us here at Dane Building Group."

Ethan forced himself to keep his expression calm. It was the first time in years his father had offered him any kind of praise, backhanded or not. It should have made him feel proud, especially considering how shitty Carson was looking.

His brother leaned forward. "This is a closed meeting."

Ethan leaned forward, eyes locked on his brother's, and took a long drink of his water. He was very aware of their father staring at the interchange, along with everyone else pretending not to stare. "I'm a shareholder."

"That's right, Carson. Ethan may also be taking over the company if his proposal is as good as I expect it will be."

Carson looked as though his head was about to explode. If he liked his brother more, he'd almost feel bad for him. Their father was really a disloyal manipulator.

Carson leaned back in his chair and spoke a little too loudly. "Well, that's if he can manage all that. We all know he must be busy with all his doctor's appointments."

He eyed Carson's chair and decided it wouldn't tip over easily.

"I'm sure he'll manage, he always does. I'm glad you joined us today, Ethan. I was going to call and invite you to the club tonight for dinner. Seven o'clock."

Of course it was assumed that he'd say yes. His father hadn't even asked, just commanded. He wasn't Carson. As much as he was jealous of Carson, he wasn't him. "Thanks for the invitation, but I have plans." Much better plans.

Carson choked on his coffee. Their father nodded stiffly but didn't say a word, and soon the meeting started. He sat there, thinking how crazy this all was. He'd thought he'd get some sort of high by being here and screwing with Carson's head, but he didn't. Nothing compared to how he felt when he was around Allie.

Hell. This day was going to hell, and it wasn't over yet. It had started out so promising—ambushing the meeting, watching Carson squirm, having their father openly favor him…but instead he was left with a crappy feeling in the pit of his stomach. He found himself rotting in guilt because of Allie and the shelter.

Ethan slammed his phone down on his desk and stared out the window. No one was home. Allie was working late, and Dani was wherever it was teenagers went close to the weekend.

He didn't know how he was going to face Allie tonight. Or tomorrow. Or any day, unless some kind of miracle happened. Since he didn't believe in those, he was SOL.

The phone rang and he picked it up, hoping that maybe it was his office with some kind of good news. He had already touched base with his lawyer and good friend, Nicholas Wright, and started the ball rolling on finding a different property for the shelter. If he couldn't keep the shelter open in that location, then he needed to work on Plan B. So far, the problem was that all the suitable properties were too distant from the city. Not at all what Allie wanted.

"Hello, Mr. Dane, this is Julie at Dr. Peterson's office. I wanted to let you know that your appointment scheduled for December first has been rescheduled for the fifth."

Ethan ran his free hand down his face. "That's not going to work for me, Julie."

"I'm sorry, but Dr. Peterson's on vacation until then. It's only a few days."

"These appointments are scheduled in advance. I did the scan and blood work six weeks ago."

"Maybe I could check and see if another doctor can see you. It's just for results so—"

"No, I don't want to see another doctor. I'll see Dr. Peterson on the fifth then."

"Thank you, Mr. Dane. The appointment is for three p.m."

"Fine." He hung up the phone, not in the mood for pleasantries. He made the adjustments to his calendar, and then chucked his red pen on the desk. He stood, letting his chair roll along the hardwood and crash against the wall a few seconds later. Walking over to his bookshelf, he stared at the picture that had been with him since he was a kid. He picked it up, frowning as he looked at the kids in it. Sometimes it felt as though it had never happened, that he wasn't that kid, that he didn't know those people. Sometimes he felt like he still *was* that kid, that he would forever be that kid. That kid had been fearless at one time. He glanced over at the small, wooden box on his desk, contemplating opening it. He knew what was inside. He opened it once a year, put the contents in his pocket, and took it with him to his doctor's appointment. It was his good luck charm—not that he'd ever admit that kind of sappy weakness aloud. The objects inside were given to him by two of the most important females in his life at one point. He allowed himself to think of them this time of year, and then he was better off just pushing their memory aside for the rest of it.

He put the silver-rimmed picture down, his fingers leaving prints on the polished frame. He wasn't going to open the box. Another two weeks. He'd have to wait two weeks for sanity. Two weeks to pretend like he was this normal guy that was worthy of being Allie's friend. And now he knew for sure he couldn't give in to the attraction he felt for her. Allie needed a guy with solid principles, who didn't give a rat's ass about revenge. And she certainly didn't need a guy who was weak.

He walked out of the room. He needed to run.

A llie walked past the corridor that led to Ethan's private wing; she slowed her steps. She glanced down the end of the hall, where the room to his home gym was half open. He never left his doors open, but then he wasn't expecting her home now. He probably thought he was here by himself. The pounding of footsteps on a treadmill seemed loud in the empty condo.

She knew she was here because she wanted to talk to him, which was crazy. She wanted his support, to see his eyes soften with concern, hear that gravelly, intimate tone of his voice when he spoke to her. She was starting to lean on him, and as scary as that was for her, she couldn't help it. Her entire life she'd been alone, and she was a single parent to her teenage sister, but living here with Ethan made her feel not so alone, made her crave...him.

She slowly walked toward the sound. Maybe she'd close the door for him. Pausing outside the room, she fought the urge to peek inside. *Close the door and walk away, Allie.* Except she caught a flash of movement and bare skin. Curiosity won and she glanced through the opening and she felt her jaw disengage. Ethan didn't jog; Ethan *ran.* Long, powerful strides that made it obvious he was in here every day. His shirt was off, draped on the handlebars. Sweat dripped down his torso, and she stared like a kid in a candy store at the ripple of perfect muscle, the taut, rock-hard stomach, the sheer masculine beauty that she had always pictured under his clothes. Yes, mouthwatering, except for the look on his face. He looked as though he was running with a purpose, away from something. The veins in his neck were strained, the lean lines of his face pulled tight. His expression was grim, determined.

She backed away, feeling like an intruder. It looked personal, his run. She pulled the door shut slowly, hoping he wouldn't notice her. The door to his office was open, and what was it with her today? She was not a nosy person, but there was another side of him, almost like he had a whole other life.

She should keep walking back to her room. Unfortunately her feet didn't get the memo, and she walked into his office. Like the rest of the condo, it was immaculate—dark floors and dark, masculine furniture. This room also had a view of the city along one wall. There was a fireplace with a thick, mahogany mantle flanked by stunning, floor-to-ceiling, built-in, mahogany bookcases. Ethan's desk was neat, his laptop shut in the middle.

She walked over to admire the bookcases. Her fingers ran over the spines of the books, taking in the titles. She paused, her gaze scanning the titles again. She took a step back from the shelf, the vast number of books with the same theme finally registering. Her stomach dropped faster than an elevator in free fall as an idea percolated. The one word that was a constant in all the titles sent a chill down her spine that she couldn't shrug. Cancer.

What did that mean? Why would Ethan have over two dozen books on the subject? That went beyond just human interest, unless maybe one of his parents had been diagnosed and he was doing research. But then the image of him and the crazy smoothies Dani teased him about appeared. And the highly controlled way he ate, the resolution to only allow himself sugar in December. And the way she'd just witnessed him running.

She folded her arms under her breasts. Maybe these were all isolated habits. Maybe none of them had to do with anything other than a highly disciplined lifestyle. She looked up and her heart stopped for a brief second as her gaze landed on a picture of a little boy and girl. Her hand shook slightly as she picked up the picture. The little girl was smiling, but her face was pale and she had a Mickey Mouse scarf around her head, which appeared to be bald underneath. She was dressed in a hospital gown. The little boy beside her was Ethan, it had to be. His eyes were unmistakable, and the way they looked into the camera…she knew that boy. He was smiling at the camera as well, his arm was around the girl, and he was wearing a hospital gown and a matching handkerchief around his head. Her entire body tingled with goose bumps and dread.

"Shoot," she mumbled, wiping away a few tears that dropped onto the glass. She bit her lower lip and blinked until she got herself together. She was jumping to conclusions. She was invading his privacy, but she couldn't look away from the little boy.

She looked over at his empty desk, picturing him there. Handsome, charming, controlled. He embodied health and virility. No, this was all just random coincidence. Her gaze went to the desk calendar and the red circles in early December. She glanced at the doorway, making sure no one was coming, and then tiptoed over to the desk, still clutching the picture to her chest. There were scratches and indiscernible words on December first. But inside the circle on December fifth were the words "D-Day" in his handwriting. What did that mean?

The frame slipped out of her fingers and tumbled onto the desk, knocking open a small box. She scrambled, quickly trying to put the lid back on the box while swearing at her stupidity. A small, handwritten note and a worn, paper hospital identity bracelet inside the box stopped her. Her heart was beating painfully now, and she knew she was a total emotional wreck. She shouldn't be doing this, she was not a snoop, but all this stuff was making itself so accessible, like the universe was deciding she needed to know this about him and…she was terrified of what this meant about Ethan.

She ignored the tremor in her hand and picked up the hospital bracelet. The typed letters were faded but she could still make them out: CARA BRONS DOB 07.08.1982, THE HOSPITAL FOR SICK KIDS. She tried swallowing as she quickly returned the bracelet and picked up the note, closing her eyes as she recognized the familiar words of the serenity prayer. How many times had she recited those words? How many times had she taught them to the kids at the shelter? How many times had she begged her mother to truly live by those words? Who had given this to Ethan? Who was Cara Brons?

"Looking for something?"

Allison jumped, the paper falling onto the desk, and looked in the direction of the voice. Ethan, standing in the doorway, sweat clinging to every perfectly sculpted muscle. She quickly wiped the tears off her face and grabbed the paper, dropping it into the box, fumbling to shut the lid. She looked over at him, very aware that he hadn't made a sound but was watching her.

He was holding a towel, wearing only his running shorts, still breathing deeply from his run. After her sad lack of discipline in staring at his body, she finally raised her eyes to his and they were devoid of the usual sparkle. Or heat. Instead, they were sharp, accusing, not an ounce of warmth in their brown depths, or in him as he strode across the room, stopping inches from her. She tried to keep her eyes on his, but she couldn't take the anger there. She focused on a small freckle on the top of his well-developed shoulder.

"What are you doing?"

She cleared her throat, trying to stop the panic that was filling her. Panic at being caught? This wasn't normal panic. This was…

"I took you and your sister in, Allie, with only one stipulation: stay out of my office."

"I know, I don't know what…" Her voice trailed off because the only answer she had would have been pure crap. She had been nosy, and then curious, and then concerned. None of those would have been the right answer. Under normal circumstances she would be able to talk her way out of this, but nothing was normal about what she'd uncovered.

She glanced at his face, and her stomach stirred with dread. His mouth was drawn into a tight line, and he looked as pissed as she'd ever seen him. Ethan was never angry. He never lost his cool. Except now. Her gaze went to his hair, thick and mussed up. Then she thought of the picture, the little boy without hair, and she wanted to cry. He must have sensed her sympathy because his jaw began that clench that indicated he was still pissed.

"It's, um, a really nice office."

His gaze went to the picture on the desk, and she cursed herself for walking around with it. "I, um, just, I was looking and this kind of fell into my hands." She tried to back up a step from him and ended up bumping into his desk, and then sitting on a stapler. She yelped and jumped up, only to crash into him. Good grief. Then she made the mistake of placing her hands on his hot, tight skin. He was strong. He was healthy. Ethan was *fine.*

"You should probably go shower and, uh, I'll just—"

"Not be nosy?"

She frowned. "I get you're mad at me, but I wasn't nosy, I was concerned for you."

"Really?"

She nodded, not getting why he was still engaging her in conversation when it was clear he was so royally pissed at her. She tried to concentrate on his eyes and not the body that was almost naked in front of her. "Yes, you're a good friend."

"Ah, yes, because we can never be anything more."

"I didn't say that."

"Really, 'cause I thought you said that. On at least three different occasions."

"Why do I get the feeling you're setting me up here?"

"What do you mean?"

"You don't want anything to do with me. If you did, you wouldn't be standing here being all scary," she said, waving her hand around.

He ran his hands down his face, moving away from her. "Just do me a favor and get out, okay?"

She winced at the carefully controlled rage in his deep voice and nodded repeatedly, walking across the room. She stopped at the doorway and turned around to look at him. His head was downturned, staring at his desk calendar. His broad shoulders looked stiff, the muscles in his arms taut. She should say something, anything to lighten the mood. Or apologize. "I'm sorry," she said. And then waited. But painfully awkward seconds went by and he said nothing, so she left the room, closing the door quietly behind her.

She had blown it, had completely invaded his privacy. They probably never should have stayed with him. It was time for them to leave. This was the second blow of the day, Ethan shutting her down, making it clear that they were nothing more than casual friends. She couldn't even fault him, but she could leave.

He was the worst kind of asshole. He was the kind that made no sense. He wanted Allie—had wanted her for years—and then he'd treated her like shit. But he couldn't deal. He could not deal with the idea of sharing his past. He heard people in real relationships did that kind of thing. Allie would expect that kind of thing. The look in her eyes replayed in his mind all afternoon. She had been all soft and compassionate, and maybe at one time in his life he would have welcomed that, but not now. But where the hell did that leave them? Things were about to get worse, too, because he knew he was going to cancel on tonight's plans with her.

Right now he'd drown his issues in scotch with his friends. They were sitting in a booth in one of the city's restaurants. He hadn't been there before, but they'd decided to meet there because it was beside the hotel Hayden was staying in. Dark, leather booths lined the perimeter. The lighting was dim, the music was soft, but the people were loud. White Christmas lights were strung across the front windows and large, dark green, square wreaths were hung throughout. Allie would have loved it.

"So, you want a condo proposal like yesterday?"

Ethan tried to smile at his old friend, Hayden Brooks, but he was going through the motions. He was happy to catch up with his old university buddy, but he couldn't go through with this project without destroying Allie. Yeah, he wanted to beat his brother, but now there was the problem of Allie and her shelter. He was a damn liar. Promising her that he'd help her save it and then going behind her back to bid on the property. "We don't own it yet. I need a conceptual project to present to my father. I'm going up against my brother."

Hayden smiled and then signaled the waitress for a refill of his scotch. "Nothing like strong familial bonds."

"Yeah. Shackles is more like it."

"Okay, well, I already have the details you sent over. I'll

get a team on this right away. Do you have a vision?"

"No," he said flatly. The only vision he had was of Allie, telling him he was an asshole.

"I hate to ask personal questions when I'd really rather be talking about business, but you don't exactly sound like you're excited about this possible acquisition."

He leaned back in his chair, absently watching as the waitress brought his friend another drink. "I'm not. The circumstances changed, and now the last thing I want is to buy this land and build the damn condo."

Hayden leaned forward, lowering his voice in the loud restaurant. "Why?"

He scrubbed a hand down his face. "There's a shelter for teens in there right now. The landlord wants to sell out, knowing he'd make a helluva lot more to sell to a builder instead of collecting rent from them. I feel…"

"Like an asswipe for evicting kids out of a shelter?"

Ethan frowned. He didn't remember Hayden being this irritating. "Yeah, something like that. When are you going back to Vancouver?"

His friend laughed, except it sounded forced. That's when he noticed the guy had dark circles under his eyes, and he didn't look like his usual kick-ass self. He looked…stressed out or something. "I don't know. Right now I'm up shit creek, actually."

Ethan motioned to the waitress for a refill. "What's wrong?"

Hayden let out a groan and then rubbed the back of his neck. "You're not going to believe it, but I hooked up with some random woman one night. It was stupid and not something I'm in the habit—"

"You don't need to justify it."

"I can't believe what an idiot I was. Anyway, a couple of months ago she appears on my doorstep, out of the blue.

I didn't even recognize her, out of sight out of mind, you know—it was years ago. Anyway, she says I got her pregnant."

Ethan tried his best not to choke on his glass of scotch. He didn't say anything as his friend sat there looking like his entire world was crashing down around him. He guessed it probably was. Maybe he'd be looking as shitty as Hayden in a few weeks if he didn't find a way out of this mess and Allie found out what he'd been up to.

"And what happened?"

Hayden rubbed his eye sockets with the back of his hands. Jeez, this guy was in bad shape. "She said she gave the baby up for adoption."

"Shit."

"Yeah, and then she tried to blackmail me."

"What the hell?"

"The thought that I have a kid somewhere who thinks they have no parent, or no parent that wants them…shit…" Hayden choked for a moment then downed the rest of his scotch. Hell. He didn't know what to say so he ordered them another round.

"What are you going to do?"

"That's why I'm in Toronto. I've been working with a PI who's tracked her down to some little town called Still Harbor."

"I don't know what to say, man. I'm sorry."

"Yeah. It…the baby…well, kid now, is a little girl. I might have a little girl out there."

"When do you go?"

Hayden clamped his hands around his empty glass, staring at the ice. "Tomorrow."

"Well…good luck."

Hayden shrugged his shoulders, slammed his glass down a little hard, and then looked up at him, his features looking more normal. "Thanks, but never mind all that, we'll get this proposal done for you. My team is on it." He glanced down at his watch. "Isn't Jackson supposed to be here?"

"Speak of the devil," Ethan said, just as Jackson joined them. He slid into the booth beside Hayden. After they'd exchanged the appropriate back slaps and greetings, they looked over the menu.

"Hell, Jackson, why do you look so happy?"

Jackson gave one of those irritating grins he'd seemed to sport ever since getting married. "Because I am happy."

"This is a far cry from the jerk I remember from university."

Ethan threw back his head and laughed.

"That's funny, very funny. So why do you look like hell?" Jackson said, obviously just noticing how crappy their friend looked.

Hayden's face fell. "I can't talk about it again."

Ethan filled him in. "Some random chick had his baby, put it up for adoption, and is now blackmailing him."

Jackson gave a low whistle. "Hell."

"Thanks. I'm living it right now."

"And what's up with you? I leave town for two weeks and suddenly you look like the grim reaper?"

Ethan scowled at his friend. "Why are you even in town?"

"We're leaving again in the morning. Em has an ear infection, and I didn't trust those country doctors, so we decided to bring her in to the city."

"She feeling better?"

Jackson nodded. "Are Allie and her sister driving you insane?"

Yes. They were. Except he liked the insanity. He liked having Allie in his house…and Dani…and even Hook. But what he liked even more was how close he was to Allie now. Well, was. Before he shut her down.

"Or is it Hook, is he driving you nuts? Charlie doesn't

like Hook."

Hayden scowled at Jackson. "Hell, man. Are you actually discussing two dogs?"

Thank God Hayden wasn't married and could relate to the insanity that was now his best friend. He was about to agree when he caught sight of a hideous figure rounding the corner and walking toward their booth. "Shit," he said under his breath, "my brother is here." Seriously, a city of millions and he had to run into him?

Carson pulled up to their table like a slimy salesman. "Hello, gentlemen."

His friends tried to give his brother a civil welcome. "Carson."

"Ethan, I'm surprised to see you out tonight."

Ethan let out a ragged sigh. He didn't have time for this tonight. He took Jackson's full glass of scotch and took a long drink. His friend didn't even complain. "Why are you surprised?"

"Well, it's just that Mom was talking the other day —"

"I don't think Jackson and Hayden want to hear about our family business."

"Speaking of family business, how's that proposal coming along? Dad was asking about it the other day."

"Can't wait to do the presentation," Hayden interjected. He gave Carson one of his infamous, nasty smiles that had the ability to send chills down a person's spine. "How do you like the hotel?"

Ethan paused, his glass on his way to his lips, watching Carson squirm.

"What are you talking about?"

"I could have sworn I saw you checking in just as I was leaving."

God, he loved his friends.

His brother's smile dipped a notch. "Right. Well, good to

see you."

"I think your wife's leaving with another guy," Jackson said, tilting his head in the direction of the door.

His brother ran off, and the three of them laughed. His phone beeped, and he glanced at the text message. *Running late. Wait for me.* Ethan cursed and looked up at his friends.

"Looks like Nick is running late. Settle in."

They motioned to the bartender and Ethan knew he had to call Allie, if she'd even pick up the phone. He had to cancel on her.

Chapter Six

Ethan entered his condo, not really knowing what to expect. Hook came running up to him; at least the dog still liked him. It wasn't the dog he was worried about, though.

He hung his coat up and loosened his tie, noticing with a frown how quiet it was in the place. Had Allie finished wrapping everything already? And usually Dani made a racket. He walked down the hallway and stopped. He'd been planning on going into the living room, but a trail of wrapping paper led down his corridor.

He followed it and stopped at the threshold of his bedroom door. This was a sight he hadn't expected: Allie was sprawled out on his bed, sort of like a starfish. She was surrounded by gift wrap and ribbons. And wasn't he an ass? He was supposed to help her wrap all the presents for the kids, but instead he was plotting to get rid of her beloved shelter and obtain his father's company.

She gave a little moan and turned on her back, crinkling Grinch gift wrap with the movement. Amazingly, guilt didn't prevent him from admiring the woman in his bed, the only woman he'd wanted in his bed in a long, long time. Her hair was all splayed across his pillow and a few strands on her face. Her baggy reindeer bottoms hid what he knew to be an exceptional pair of legs, but her tank top revealed full breasts and a flat stomach. He ran his hands through his hair. He should leave the room, his room, which made him wonder what she was doing in here anyway, not that he was complaining.

His gaze went to his nightstand—there was a bottle of rum and a carton of organic eggnog. He smiled, and then felt guilty again. He should have been with her. She shouldn't have been wrapping presents and drinking spiked eggnog by herself.

He sat on the bed beside her. He probably should have tried to wake her and apologize, but instead he enjoyed looking at her for a moment. He'd always had an idea of the kind of person Allie was, had always been attracted to her. But living with her and really knowing her only made him want her more and want to know every little thing about her.

He lay down beside her, moving a clump of hair off her face. "Allie, it's Ethan."

She frowned but didn't open her eyes. She was probably still pissed at him.

"I'm sorry, Allie." One eye opened, looked at him, and then shut again. He smiled. "Allie, about what happened earlier…"

She waved a hand but ended up whacking him in the face. That got her attention, and she propped herself up on her elbows, her shirt stretching tautly over her breasts, which happened to look as though they would spill out of her bra at any moment. God. That was his punishment for the condo. "Sorry," she whispered, her voice husky and her words slurred. Great. Not the combination he was looking for.

"I'm the one who needs to apologize. I'm not used to

sharing."

"It's okay, you won't have to anymore," she said in some sort of sexy-yet-inebriated slur.

"What do you mean?"

"I think we'll crash at Jackson and Hannah's for a week, and by then I'll be able to find us a new apartment."

His gut turned, and he looked at the only woman he'd truly wanted and felt like shit. He was driving her out. "Allie—"

She did the arm wave again, and this time he ducked in time. "No, no, I totally imposed. It's okay, I make it a policy to always have a plan B. Seriously, what was I thinking? Me, a teenager, and a disabled dog."

"I love having you guys here." She shook her head, and for a second he thought he saw tears. Hell no, he was going to make her cry? "Allie, sweetheart, trust me, you don't want to stay with Jackson and Hannah. They have kids. You know what people with kids are like. They go to bed early, their kids wake up in the middle of the night with runny noses and ear infections, and they invite people over for brunch instead of dinner."

That earned him an adorable half-smile. "You're very charming. Have I ever told you that?" she asked in that throaty voice. Her arm went up and for a second it looked as though she was going to touch his face.

He stilled. "How much did you have to drink?"

"I used a measuring cup. I'm not usually a drinker, so it doesn't take much. But I'm totally not drunk or anything. That being said, I'm finding myself desperately needing to touch your face, Ethan," she whispered. He sat there as her arm waved slightly but then found its way to his face. Her hand clutched his cheek. He held it there, because he wasn't sure she'd be able to hold on, and he was sure he didn't want her to let go. But before he did what he'd wanted to the moment he met her, he needed to know just how drunk she was. "Also,

I need to tell you that I think you're really hot in this get-up."

"My suit?"

She bobbed her head up and down against the pillow. "But I think I really like Weekend Ethan best."

"Who?"

"Weekend Ethan. That's when you're all scruffy." She patted his face. "And so delectable I could just lick you."

He groaned; she couldn't be that drunk. He leaned down, bracing his forearms beside her head. Her pupils dilated, and her hand stayed on his face. His gaze went from her eyes to her mouth, and he couldn't believe he'd waited this long to finally kiss Allie. He lowered his mouth to hers, but she started speaking again.

"But then today you got all Abominable on me — "

He kissed her temple, trying to follow the conversation, but needing to make contact with her. "Abominable?" he murmured, placing a kiss beneath her earlobe, smiling as she sighed.

"Yeah, as in the Abominable Snowman in Rudolph. The original Rankin/Bass Rudolph."

He kissed his way back to her mouth. "I acknowledge no other Rudolph, and I was not like the Abominable Snowman. My eyes aren't googly, and I'm not that hairy."

She laughed and then placed her hands at the nape of his neck. He shifted on the bed and slid between her legs.

"I'm sorry about today, Allie," he whispered, looking in her eyes again, searching for the truth of what she saw in him. He didn't want to see pity or compassion. He couldn't handle it from Allie. He only wanted to see lust tonight.

She placed her hand on the right side of his chest. "You have a good heart, I can feel it. You're one of the good guys, and I'm so sorry for not trusting you or seeing that earlier. You took us in, and you're trying to help me save the shelter."

He would have laughed when moving her hand to the

left side of his chest, but instead guilt railroaded him. She was looking at him the way he'd always imagined, except she was seeing someone entirely different. She was seeing a sham.

"And the reason I came in here tonight was because after I was done feeling sorry for myself—rum helps with that, by the way—I thought I'd seduce you."

He stopped breathing for a moment. This was what he'd always wanted. Allie. In his life. In his bed. He battled with his conscience for a moment. She trusted him. *The shelter.* He should get up and walk out of this room. But again, because he was pretty certain this woman had set out to torture him, she began speaking. "Ethan, I've wanted you since the night of Jackson and Hannah's wedding. I've wanted you, and I was too afraid to ever take a chance with someone like you."

Hell. He was going to hell, but he'd worry about that later. There was no way he could walk away from this, from her. He was going to kiss her, except she started talking again.

"Also. You should know I'm not upset about what happened in your office today."

"You should be. I was an ass," he said, dipping his head and kissing her neck. He couldn't keep his hands off her.

"No, I get it. You have secrets. I have secrets, too," she whispered. The tone of her voice made him raise his head. Her eyes were glistening with something he didn't get. He placed his hands on either side of her face, suddenly wanting to know everything. He wished he were different. He wished he could let her in and be the man she deserved to have.

"You know you can tell me anything."

She gave her head a slight shake. "It goes both ways."

He nodded, not satisfied with that solution, but knowing it was all they had right now.

"But that doesn't mean we can't have this," she said as she tugged him down. He leaned down and kissed Allie the way he'd wanted to since the moment he met her.

Her hands tightened around his hair, and she moaned sweetly, music to his ears. He could feel her breasts, her curvy body under his, and she was better, hotter than he'd imagined. He tasted her, explored her mouth until neither of them could breathe. "I need to know how drunk you are, Allie," he said against her lips. There was no way this could go any further if she wasn't going to remember in the morning. She pulled back slightly but didn't let go of him.

"So not drunk."

He kissed her again and prayed she'd answer correctly. "What day of the week is it?"

She frowned up at him. "Christmas?"

He groaned. "Allie, please tell me you're joking." He rested his forehead against hers for a second. He felt her hands sliding off him. He lifted his head. She'd passed out.

Allie's phone started vibrating on the nightstand.

Slowly disengaging himself from the hottest woman he'd ever known and trying not to weep, he spotted Dani's face on the display of Allie's phone. He picked it up, frowning. It was almost midnight, why was she calling? Wasn't she home?

He answered the phone as quietly as he could and got up from the bed.

"Oh my God, Ethan, thank God it's you," she said. He frowned at the panic and tears he heard in her voice. He quickly covered Allie with part of the duvet and left the room.

He shut the bedroom door and walked to the front entrance. "Where are you?"

"Allie's going to kill me, promise me you won't tell."

"Tell me where you are, and I'll come and get you."

There was a huge sigh and then a long pause. Then she

named a suburb of the city. Not the nicest area by any stretch.

His stomach tightened. "How the hell did you get there?"

"With this guy. We were supposed to go this party, and he drove us out here, but it's in the sticks and there's no subway or transit. I have no way back to the city, and this party is creeping me out."

"Give me an address and I'll come and get you." He wasn't going to berate her for her utter stupidity and recklessness until he had her safely in his car. He could subject her to a half hour lecture in the car ride home, after he knew she was safe. He scribbled down the address she gave while he put on his shoes. Teenagers. How did Allie deal with this? He walked out the door while instructing her to stay on the phone with him.

"It's not that bad."

"Do you know anyone there?"

"No," she said in a small voice.

"Where's the douchebag that brought you there?"

"I don't know." Her voice was losing its bravado, and she was sounding more and more vulnerable by the minute.

"All right, well, babble about something while I get into the car. Just don't hang up the phone, hon. I'm on my way." He punched the address into his GPS and took the quickest way to the highway.

He mentally rehearsed the lecture he was about to give, while Dani blabbed about how stupid her friends were. And then every few minutes she'd beg him not to tell Allie.

"'Kay, Dani, I'm in your neighborhood. Go wait on the porch and don't talk to anyone or wander off into some dark alley or something."

"As if I'd do that. I'm not a complete moron. Ethan, is that you driving down the street?"

"I see you. I'm hanging up." He was shocked by the ferocity of the relief that barreled into him as Dani waved frantically from the street curb. He pulled the car up to her and leaned over to open the door.

She sank into the seat and threw her arms around him. "I'm so happy to see you. Thank you, Ethan." She held on to him, and he felt the tremors that ran through her. She pulled away and buckled herself in. She looked young and scared as she wrapped her arms around herself, shivering. He turned the heat on high, pulled away from the curb, and decided his lecture could wait a bit.

He glanced over at her once they were on the highway. She hadn't said a word, which was probably a record for her.

"You're not going to tell Allie, right?"

He didn't know how he was going to handle that. He didn't feel right about not telling Allie about something that happened to Dani. She wasn't his kid. He couldn't keep something like that from her. "Why don't you tell me exactly what happened tonight?"

She groaned and shut her eyes. "That's adult evasion, isn't it? You're going to tell her."

"If I were you, I'd stop worrying about that and just be happy you aren't still at that rat-hole."

"Fine. You're right. So this guy I have liked for*ever*, and who never noticed me before, asked me out."

"So why did he notice you now?"

"Because I look so much better with all the cool stuff I bought. He may have overheard me bragging about where we live now…and maybe about your Porsche."

"Sounds like a winner. Why would you even want to go out with a guy like that?"

"You wouldn't understand. You're not a girl."

"Allie's a girl. Why don't we ask her?"

"That's not funny. Besides, she never makes mistakes, and she thinks I should be perfect like her."

"I don't think so. I've never heard her say that. All I see

is a woman in her twenties who doesn't make a lot of money, took in her younger sister, puts up with all her smart-ass remarks, and pays for whatever she needs."

The sniffles he heard didn't make him feel bad. He kept his eyes on the road, his thoughts on Allie, who was trying to do everything right.

"You're right."

He shot her a side-glance. She was sitting hunched over, arms crossed, pout on her face.

"And it's even worse, what I did."

His hands clenched the leather steering wheel and braced himself. "What else did you do?"

She groaned and slouched farther into the seat. He wondered if she would slink right off the damn seat. "I got really mad at her at our mom's place."

His stomach dipped. He didn't know much about their mother except what he read between the lines. "You went to see your mother?"

"She dragged me there. She had all these presents for her and said it was Christmas and we should at least try and forgive and make peace. Or whatever."

He turned on the wipers as the snow increased. "So what happened?"

"Exactly what I knew would happen. Our mom didn't even have a Christmas card for us—and she's a hoarder. Like, what's the point of being a hoarder if you don't even have things when you need them? Oh, but she did give me some ratty, random bag of Christmas M&Ms, and there's Allie giving her presents. And the worst part? Our mom asked her for five hundred bucks because Bill the Bumpkin spent all their cash at the casino."

Ethan swore under his breath. This was all completely new to him.

"That was exactly what I thought."

"Did Allie give her the money?"

"Yup! Of course! Because Allie feels sorry for her or something."

He let out a long breath.

"So now Allie owes like half the town money. You. The bank."

He clenched his hand around the leather of the steering wheel feeling like such an ass, along with feeling horrible for her. "Allie doesn't owe me money."

"Can I get that in writing, because she made some spreadsheet with a repayment plan."

A smile tugged at the corner of his mouth. He had to respect that, even though he wouldn't accept a dime from her. "Sure. Listen, I'm sorry. That really sucks about your mom. I'm not that close to my parents so I get feeling…disappointed."

"It wasn't that. That's not what I'm so…sad about."

"Then what?"

She put her hands on her face. He awkwardly patted her on the head for a second. "I'm not Hook, Ethan."

"Well, then speak."

"I yelled at her."

"Your mom?"

"No," she whispered in this little voice that caught. He braced himself for whatever she was going to say as well as the onslaught of tears. "I yelled at Allie in front of our mom. I called her weak and spineless and told her I had no respect for her."

Oh, man. He barely understood the female mind, but the teenage female mind was even more daunting. He cleared his throat and patted her on the head again until she swatted his hand away. "Did you apologize?"

She shook her head.

"So you yelled at your sister who took you in, and provides you with a home, food, and clothes. Then you refused to help her wrap gifts for a bunch of homeless kids and snuck out with a guy who she forbid you to see."

"It gets worse."

He resisted the urge to swear out loud. "How?"

She slumped her head against the window and sniffled. "Allie never tells me stuff. She always tries to pretend that everything's fine and under control, even when our apartment burned down. It's like she doesn't want me to worry. But then, after I yelled at her…she tried telling me stuff, like why she would give our mom money. It was bad. She started saying something like she owed our mom, because there was a time our mom rescued her." She stopped speaking abruptly and groaned.

He couldn't deal with the dread. "Come on, what else?"

"She started saying something about this guy coming into her room at night."

This time he did swear, immediately thinking about Allie lying in his bed, looking up at him, telling him that she had secrets, too. God, this better not be what it was sounding like.

"I know, it's so bad and I feel so bad for her, but I made it worse because I didn't let her tell me. I acted like a baby and covered my ears and ran away. Allie never tells me things. She does everything on her own, solves every problem on her own, she solves other people's problems, but no one ever helps her. The one time she trusts me and I totally bailed."

Ethan absently tried patting Dani's head again, but she swatted him away. He was too busy trying to process what she'd told him. Allie was this woman who had everything together on the outside, but inside she was still dealing with baggage and pain from her past. She trusted him. He had failed her. Today in his office. Tonight with the presents. Not to mention the shelter. When the hell had everything become so damn complicated?

"Well, aren't you going to say anything?" Dani screeched.

He tried to concentrate on Dani while still processing what she'd revealed about Allie.

"It's not your fault you couldn't deal with what she said."

"Of course it is."

"I'm sure she doesn't blame you. Just try not to be so selfish all the time."

"Are you trying to make me pitch myself from this rapidly moving vehicle?"

"No, I'm trying to make sure you feel guilty enough so you get your head out of your ass and start showing Allie the respect she deserves. And yourself. It's time you started appreciating the life you have and making it the best of what you get."

She didn't say anything for a few minutes, then she leaned forward and tuned the radio to some Christmas carols. "You're right, and I was thinking I should get a job. I know Allie keeps telling me I should concentrate on school so I can get a scholarship—and I do—I totally do and I have good grades, but I should do more."

He resisted the urge to grin. "Good. So when we get back you're going to show me how to wrap presents."

"What?"

"You and I have to wrap the gifts for the kids at the shelter."

"I thought Allie was going to do that."

The image of Allie passed out on his bed with eggnog and rum popped into his head. "We both promised her we'd helped, and we didn't. We both bailed. So now we finish."

"She's not done?"

"She…fell asleep. With rum and eggnog."

"Allie doesn't drink."

He glanced over at her. "Really?"

She nodded. "Yeah, because our mom…drinks too much. I've seen Allie drink maybe a half glass of wine when friends are over, but never by herself."

Ah, hell. Now he felt even worse. He wasn't there for her on a bad day. He had made it worse. That wasn't what he wanted. That wasn't the guy he wanted to be. He wanted Allie for real. He wanted to be there for her, every day.

Allie woke to the sound of muffled cursing, then the crumpling of paper, followed by more cursing. She slowly opened her eyes and sought out the display on the alarm clock, but it wasn't where it was supposed to be. She frowned, realizing she wasn't in her bed, or her room. She opened her eyes abruptly and was gifted with the sight of Ethan. He must have been getting ready for work. His hair was wet, and he was pulling a red bow off the bottom of his sock and holding a coffee mug in the other hand. The cursing resumed when coffee sloshed over the rim and on to the carpet as he walked over and placed the cup on the nightstand beside her.

Her drooling ceased immediately as she realized that she'd passed out in his room due to spiked eggnog intoxication and self-pity when he hadn't shown up last night. She cursed herself for being naive and thinking he'd want to spend an evening with her wrapping presents. Of course he wouldn't. This guy could be doing anything or anyone in the entire city. Why would he want to spend any night wrapping gifts and drinking eggnog? And what really sucked was that she now had to spend the entire morning wrapping presents. She tried to close her eyes and pretend she was still sleeping until he left for work. She couldn't deal with him this morning.

"Morning, Allie."

She kept her eyes shut.

"I'm sorry about last night. I'm not sure how much you remember of our conversation, but the dinner meeting ran late and I couldn't get out of it."

She opened one eye at the mention of a conversation. She racked her brain and she had some vague recollection of him lying down beside her…and she'd hit him. She tried not to groan out loud at her humiliation. He was leaning on the dresser, fully dressed, completely gorgeous. His hair was still damp, slightly disheveled, and she tried not to imagine what it would be like if she could walk up to him and kiss him. Maybe she'd straighten his blue silk tie, hold on to the lapels of his suit and laugh, tossing her hair back at some wonderful compliment he gave her. She'd be like a woman in the movies with the handsome, successful man. She caught sight of her legs. Reindeer flannel.

She tried to inconspicuously wipe the drool off the side of her mouth as she attempted a graceful movement into a seated position. She took a moment to smooth her crazy hair off her face and make sure all parts of her were still inside her tank top. Yes, she'd worn the gorgeous pink push-up bra and matching underwear, not that it had mattered. It really was the seduction ensemble of a chicken. The flannel had been in case he turned her down—she wouldn't have looked like she had intentionally been trying to seduce him. The push-up bra and matching underwear had been in case something had happened. She waved a hand and tried not to look as though it was a big deal. She had no recollection of a conversation, and that was slightly disconcerting. It couldn't have lasted very long if she didn't even remember it.

"I don't remember you coming home at all."

"Oh, I was here, and you were very aware of me."

Her eyes narrowed as she detected the trace of humor laced through his voice. She sat up and took a sip of perfectly brewed coffee. He was currently rubbing his jaw and looking at her like he wanted to laugh…or inhale her for breakfast. Both those thoughts were more than a little alarming. Her gaze wandered over his face, admiring how good he looked.

He braced his arms on either side of the dresser, leaning against it and looking at her. "I just finished shaving."

"That's great…" she said, her voice trailing. She felt like she was missing something this morning. Maybe the jolt of caffeine would help her memory. She gulped some more of the hot coffee. "The last thing I remember was…enjoying some eggnog…then coming in here to hide from Hook, because he goes crazy with wrapping paper."

"That's the *only* reason you were in here?"

She hid her face in the mug of coffee, while trying to analyze whether or not she detected something suspicious in his tone. "Of course."

"Allie, I'm sorry I bailed last night."

"No worries, I know you're busy. Hannah's always telling me how busy Jackson is." But Jackson never broke dinner engagements with his wife, and if he said he'd be somewhere, he always was. There was a look in Ethan's brown eyes, like maybe he was thinking the same thing. Or maybe not. Maybe she was crazy. She was Ethan's friend. Obviously nothing close to a wife, nothing even close to someone truly significant in his life.

"Still, I told you I'd be here and I wasn't."

He walked forward slowly, and her heart increased rhythm with every assured step he took. She tried to smooth her hair, but it was so bad that her hand got tangled in a knot. A corner of his perfect mouth tugged in what she would describe as an affectionate smile. Affectionate seemed right, sort of the way he looked at Hook when he couldn't quite make the jump to the couch. Ethan was looking at her the way he looked at her one-eyed dog.

"And about yesterday in my office. I'm sorry. I overreacted."

She glanced away from his intense stare. "That's fine.

Thank you. You don't need to apologize. You told me to stay out of those rooms, and I didn't. I understand that you were upset by the invasion of privacy. I mean, you and I are just friends. Friends who don't share things about their personal lives. It's for the best really. You have my word, I'll never go into your office again."

"Allie," he groaned.

"No, no. It's really no biggie. I mean, it's not like you let other people go in there, like Berta, your cleaning lady."

He rubbed his hands over his face. "Berta doesn't read English."

"Well, regardless, I entered your secret, private lair."

He let out some strangled sort of noise. "You can go in there. Whenever you want. I'm sorry."

Now she did look up at him. He looked all brooding, not the mischievous Ethan. This was that other side of him she was getting glimpses of. She tried to make out his expression. "But you don't want me in there. Or anyone."

His broad shoulders rose and fell slightly. "I'm not used to having people around here. It wasn't personal."

She thought of the calendar, the little girl, the "D-Day." She studied his face, the closed-off expression. While the man looked like a gorgeous fortress of solitude, there was a hint of vulnerability. She had seen that look on the toughest of teenage boys that came into the shelter. There was some kind of pain beneath this facade he was wearing. No, she wouldn't ask him, not now, maybe not ever. Whatever he was hiding, he obviously didn't want to share it with her.

She forced a cheery smile on her face. "Well, no worries. I won't go in there again. In fact, we're not going to be a bother at all. I'm sure we'll be out of here in a week, tops."

"You'll go insane at Jackson and Hannah's. It's like a daycare center in there."

"Maybe we'll go to our mom's." Not that they would, but

she needed to say something.

"No you won't," he said with an edge to his voice. What was that all about? He didn't know much about their mother.

"Well, then my friend—"

"At least stay until the holidays are over."

Why was he saying this stuff to her? Why was he so impossibly put together and perfect? He had even apologized and acted like he really regretted everything from the day before.

"I wish I didn't have to go into the office," he said, his voice low and thick with something other than platonic affection. It stirred something low in her belly. She cleared her throat and attempted conversation as he loomed over her, all casual, hands in his pants pockets. Saying that he didn't want to go to the office implied he wanted to be here, with her. And her dog. And her crazy sister—

"Oh my God, did Dani come home last night?" She bolted out of the bed and almost fell over the hems of her too-long pajamas. Of course, Ethan's large hands were immediately on her shoulders, steadying her.

"Yeah. She's fine."

Allie breathed a sigh of relief. "I can't believe I didn't wake up. I knew she was mad at me."

"She's not anymore."

She rolled her eyes. "I can't keep up with her moods…uh, sorry I hijacked your bed. Where did you sleep?" She knew he couldn't have slept with her, because she had been sprawled across the middle of the bed, on a diagonal, like some sort of beached whale. No, dolphin. Yes, dolphin was much better.

He shrugged. "No worries. I didn't sleep much last night. I caught a few hours on the couch."

"Oh. I guess you were out pretty late?"

He shifted his eyes from her. She didn't know if it was from guilt or from the crazy picture she must make. She also didn't want to ask who he was out with. Even though he said it was for work, did he go out after? "Yeah. Anyway, Allie, I gotta get to work. I hope you don't have too much of a hangover today." He tilted his head toward the eggnog and rum bottles on the nightstand and gave her a slow grin.

She cleared her throat. "I should be fine. I think the eggnog does a good job of absorbing the alcohol. But I need to get going, too."

He gave her a nod and left the room. As she watched him leave, she wondered how and when this had happened. Things had never been awkward. Conversation had never been stilted, with the pauses seeming more and more uncomfortable. She waited until she heard the front door close and then ran into the main room, ready to tackle the gifts. She skidded to a stop, her bare feet squeaking on the polished wood floor at the sight in front of her—her sister was passed out on the sofa in a blanket of bows and ribbons. The coffee table, chairs, and carpet were filled with wrapped gifts. Shock made her stand there a few more minutes. Dani had done all this? She walked forward slowly, and Hook ran up to greet her.

"Hook, what happened here last night? A Christmas miracle?"

His tail wagged.

She picked up a red ribbon and dangled it around her sister's nose, tickling her with it. Dani gave a theatrical moan and threw her hand across her forehead. "Your rich boyfriend is a slave driver."

She dropped the ribbon. "What?"

Dani's eyes opened and went into immediate scowl mode. "I bought you hot pajamas so you wouldn't humiliate yourself with reindeer. No wonder Ethan won't make a move."

"Never mind that. Tell me what you meant about being a slave driver."

She swung her arm wide at the direction of the presents.

"He was guilt-ridden over not getting home in time so he made me spend the night helping him wrap these presents."

Her heart squeezed until she couldn't breathe. "You're kidding."

"I wish I were kidding. And the man has never even wrapped his own presents. For a guy who's supposed to be some sort of genius, he's a real idiot. He couldn't figure out how to keep the paper from wrinkling at the corners. The tutorial session took over half an hour."

Allie's gaze went from her sister to the pile of gifts. "It did?"

Dani stood, perching her hands on her hips. "Ethan's an okay guy. You should try and not screw things up." With those wise words her sister proceeded to exit the room but halted at the door. "Oh, and I'm sorry about what I said to you last night." She looked down at her feet. "And I'm sorry about what I said to you at Mom's. I was pissed, and I didn't mean it…and I'm sorry I acted like a baby. If you want to ever, um, talk to me, I totally want to be there for you. I really…love you."

Allie's jaw dropped open, but before she could run across the room to hug her sister, Dani had already left.

Chapter Seven

Allie hung around the front desk chatting with Denise and pretending that she wasn't nervous. Or anxious. Or excited. All because Ethan would be arriving at any moment to pick her up and go tree hunting. All she had thought about that day was how he was turning out to be this really complex guy she couldn't figure out. He wasn't who she thought he was. Rich, handsome, playboy Ethan she could easily dismiss. Gorgeous Ethan with more layers than a decadent chocolate cake was no longer dismissible, especially since she'd started having flashbacks of Ethan kissing her in his bed last night. Obviously that hadn't happened, because he would have said something. Right?

She spotted Ethan's SUV as he parked in front of their building. Ethan had obviously gone home to change. He was wearing worn-in jeans that hugged his lean hips and hung a little low, enough that the navy Henley he wore under his unbuttoned jacket clung to his flat abs and made him look like a poster boy for going to the gym. She knew he took his health seriously. He worked out at home every morning.

Saturday mornings he ran outside with a ratty old Toronto Blue Jays baseball cap and an unshaven face. She found him extra scrumptious on Saturdays and Sundays because he didn't shave. Not that it should matter to her. She adored "Weekend Ethan," which was how she thought of him.

"Oh my God, *who* is that and why is he walking in here?"

Allie smiled as she buttoned up her coat. Denise was half-standing behind the desk and watching Ethan through the large front window. "That's my friend Ethan who took Dani and me in after the fire."

"You're joking," Denise said, leaning over the desk. "Why didn't I know you have a friend like that?"

"And what would you have done with the knowledge?"

"I would have dressed a little nicer. Maybe brush my hair, put on makeup, wear pants that don't have an elastic waistband."

Allie laughed and paused for a moment, watching him through the window, too. He was on his phone, scowling at the moment. Even with a scowl the man was beautiful.

"Please tell me there's something going on with you two."

Allie pulled on her tuque, suddenly wondering about her hat choice today. "Nothing. We're just friends."

Denise groaned. "C'mon, Allie. He's perfect."

She leaned against the desk, feeling overheated, knowing it wasn't because of her coat. "You don't know anything about him. He's not really the kind of guy to settle down."

"That can be changed with the right woman. What's he doing here?"

"We're going to get a real tree for the party tonight."

Denise gave her a slow smile and leaned back in her swivel chair. "Your suggestion?"

"His."

Denise's smile grew wider.

"And...he's the guy who's going to see if he can help save

this place…somehow."

Denise's coffee sloshed over her mug. "Him? He can do that? He has that kind of power?"

"Okay, relax. First off, there's probably nothing he can do. I'm sure he's going to make a few calls and that's about it, which is very nice of him, but I'm not holding out hope. He can't stop the landlord from selling this place, or stop zoning from allowing condos to go here."

Denise looked out the window again. "Look at that power, the way he's yelling at whoever he's talking to. That is a man who can make change happen."

"No more daytime TV for you. Quiet, he's walking in," Allie whispered as Ethan turned to walk inside. He opened the door and stepped into the entryway, smiling when he saw her. It was a smile that even she couldn't deny was pretty heart-stopping.

"Hey, Allie."

"Hi. Ethan, this is my friend and the woman who runs this whole place, Denise."

Allie tried not to laugh as Denise stood and knocked over her mug of coffee as she tried to shake Ethan's hand. Charmer that the man was, he instantly went over to help her.

Five minutes later they were exiting the shelter and making their way outside. She wanted to stop him and thank him for last night, but she knew Denise was spying on them. Ethan was also acting slightly shut off. Maybe he didn't have time for this, or maybe it had occurred to him how much he'd been wasting since she had come barging into his life. And really, it was true.

Since she and Dani railroaded him, he'd had to dish out lots of money, they had taken over his apartment, her ill-trained dog insisted on sprawling himself out wherever, and now he was doing volunteer work. She was asking too much of him. There was no one in her entire life that had done this much for her, ever.

She glanced over at him, the silence in the car starting to get to her. His profile took her breath away and made it so obvious to her that this was all wrong. Ethan was going to get tired of them and tell her to leave, or to stop pestering him. She had never leaned on someone so much in her adult life.

Ethan turned down a dirt road, following the wooden arrow signs on the side of the road. A thick, heavy coating of pristine snow blanketed the rolling hills, and they rode in silence. After a few minutes a big red barn, a beaten old fence, and a dirt driveway came into view. He'd been trying to concentrate on Allie, but his mind was still on the phone call he'd taken outside the shelter. Things were not looking good. This morning he'd had the brilliant idea to see if he could get his father to find a new location for the condo. He had actually tried to appeal to the man's softer side. The only problem was his father didn't have one. He also couldn't care less that the kids in the shelter would be uprooted—he told Ethan that was on the landlord's conscience, not his. Great.

His life was suddenly complicated and filled with lies thanks to the gorgeous woman currently sitting beside him. Allie was actually at the root of all his problems. Now that he'd kissed her, he wanted her more than ever. Everything she'd revealed last night stuck to him and haunted him. What was he going to do with that knowledge? How the hell could he possibly move forward with her while lying to her?

"Everything okay?"

He glanced at Allie, and his gut churned. She thought he was a good friend. She thought he was going to help her save Haven House when he was going to be doing the opposite. She was looking at him with those eyes that had always had the power to reel him in, right from the first night he'd met her. She had walked down the aisle of the small chapel where Jackson and Hannah were married, and he'd wanted her instantly. Of course, his best friend had told him she was too nice for him, hands off. Hell, Jackson had been right.

Ethan turned to her when she gasped. "This place is just as special as I remember it. So charming!"

He smiled at the expression on her face. "When was the last time you were here?"

Her cheeks flushed almost imperceptibly. "I used to date the owner."

He didn't say anything for a moment and then looked out the windshield. He didn't see anything special about the place, just a giant barn with twinkling white lights and fresh cedar garland, a picket fence with more garland, a nice dusting of white snow, rolling hills, and a vintage Santa sled out front. Nothing special at all.

"Really? I expected the owner to be some old farmer guy."

She shot him an adorable smile. "He inherited it from his grandparents."

"Huh. Well, I guess we should go in." So a part of him really wanted to meet this guy. Another part of him had no intention of meeting him, whoever this blueberry farmer was.

He pulled into a parking spot, and Allie jumped out of the car before he had even turned off the ignition. He walked over to meet her; she looked ready to run toward the barn. There was a big sign, BLUEBERRY FARMS, hanging over the door. He had to admit the place had a certain charm to it. The escarpment in the distance was covered in snow, and the wood fence looked as though it went on for miles. The air was fresh and crisp, and even if you didn't like the cold, you couldn't knock the appeal of the area. But the nicest thing in his opinion was the woman next to his SUV. Allie's eyes were sparkling, her mouth pulled into a smile as though she was anticipating great things. That mouth. He couldn't get over their kiss, the feel of her under him. The sounds. Weekend Ethan. Wanting to lick his face. The fact that she had wanted him just as long as he'd wanted her.

"Ethan, are you sure you're feeling okay?"

He needed to focus. "Yeah, fine. Just thinking about work." And last night. And the shelter. And Allie's past with her mother. And D-Day. When did his life go from perfectly orderly to completely insane?

He grabbed her hand in his, because despite everything he couldn't not touch her anymore. She didn't pull away. Instead, she walked with him in silence. Their boots crunched against the hard packed earth. He held open the door for her, the aroma of freshly baked pastries slamming into them.

"Oh my God, this place gets better and better," Allie said, squealing. She clutched his arm and squeezed. "Come this way." She yanked him by the hand into the bakery. A massive display of every kind of imaginable dessert was showcased behind the glass. "I don't even know what to get."

"I think the Christmas trees are outside."

She shot him a look. "First we need coffee and something from the display. Gingerbread men…or look at those muffins…or those cookies. Cookies. I'm getting two cookies. Do you know what you want?" She turned to look up at him, and he had to stifle his grin. She looked like a kid.

They walked up to the cash register and Allie ordered two snowflake cookies and a coffee.

"I'll have a coffee, too," he said to the cashier and gave her the appropriate bills.

Allie frowned at him when the cashier went to retrieve their order. "Why aren't you getting anything?"

He shrugged. "I just feel like a coffee."

He grabbed their coffees and she took her bag of cookies.

"Let's sit over there," he said, pointing to a table by the window. It overlooked the fields behind the barn.

Her bag crinkled as she pulled out a white cookie and then glared at him before taking a bite. "I thought you loved cookies. Hannah dubbed you the Cookie Monster of Christmas."

He smiled and leaned back in his chair. He knew Jackson's wife had given him that name after he'd inhaled dozens of her homemade cookies one Christmas. Allie closed her eyes and moaned. Holy hell. She was crunching on that cookie like it was a sexual experience. He shifted in his chair and took a sip of coffee, burning himself on the black liquid.

"I feel bad eating if you're not."

He shrugged. "Why? Eat. Enjoy."

She finished inhaling one and was eyeing the other one in the bag. After a minute, she closed the bag with a sigh and took a sip of coffee.

"Seriously, Allie, if you want the other one eat it."

"No, no. It's okay. Why don't I save it for you on the drive back?"

"I'm not going to eat it."

"I never realized you were so anal about your weight."

"It doesn't have to do with weight."

"Dani thinks your smoothies are diet shakes."

He sighed and drank more coffee. "I don't have body issues. I just don't eat sugar until December. Then I eat it nonstop until January first."

"Why?"

"Self-discipline."

Now her eyes narrowed into slits. "Implying I have none?"

He coughed. What the hell had he gotten himself into? "No. I read a bunch of studies on sugar and decided to give it up for most of the year."

She stuffed her cookie bag into her purse and crossed one

leg over the other, swinging it in some weird rigid motion. She was pissed at him, or embarrassed maybe. "I think we should hurry up and find a tree. I heard the weather forecast, and they're calling for snow later on." She stood abruptly, almost knocking over their coffees as she swung her purse over her shoulder.

He steadied them and picked them up as he stood.

"Thank you," she said, pursing her lips and taking hers.

"Allie," he groaned, walking beside her. They exited the bakery and walked out into the fresh, cold air. The sky was gray and heavy, the air damp, and it felt like snow was coming.

She didn't say a word as they walked to the area that had rows and rows of Christmas trees. The ground beneath them was cold and bumpy, but Allie marched on until they were farther and farther from the main barn. She zigzagged through the trees and all the while mumbled and grumbled. "So I think we need something kind of like this," she said, stopping abruptly by a short, somewhat thin tree.

He made a face. "Not big enough. Too Charlie Brown. Let's go over there." He pointed to where it looked like the largest trees were displayed.

He heard Allie grumble something as he led the way. Snow started falling, and he had to admit the place would look pretty damn magical if he were one to think of magic and Christmas trees. He wasn't. She shoved him out of the way and ran past him to the largest tree in the bunch. She stood triumphantly beside it like she had won some kind of contest. She was pretty damn cute. The tip of her nose was pink, as were her cheeks. She was wearing a pale blue hat with white snowflakes and a navy coat. He wanted to haul her up to him and kiss her, but he had to remember he couldn't have anything with Allie other than friendship—and even that was soon to be doubtful if he didn't find a way to save her shelter.

"This is it, the perfect tree."

He forced his gaze from her to take in the tree. "Are you sure that's going to fit in the room?"

She frowned and assessed the tree, one hand on her hip. "Yup, totally. If you think you can manage it."

"Me? Of course. You don't have to worry about that."

She smiled smugly. "Perfect. We should probably go find out how much this costs."

"I'll cover it."

"We have enough in the budget."

"Take it and spend it on something else."

She gave him a gorgeous smile, and he grinned in return. Like a sap. He was turning into Jackson. He was smiling whenever he was around Allie. "The kids will love this."

And her, too. He wanted her to love it, too. Ah, hell, how were all these crazy thoughts creeping in? Last night had ruined him. He never should have kissed her.

"I've never had a real tree before. It smells so good." She stuck her head between a couple of branches before yelping. "Kind of prickly."

He walked over, tossing his empty coffee cup in a nearby bin. "Real trees look the best, smell the best, and don't compare to fake."

She took a sip of coffee before looking up at him. "So you had real trees growing up?"

He nodded. "Yeah, a few."

"Oh, wow. Like in different rooms?"

He stuffed his hands in his pockets. "Yeah. They were decorated according to the room they were in."

"That must have been a lot of work for your family."

He stared at her for a moment before answering. "We didn't do it ourselves. The decorators did it every year."

"Oh."

"What about you?"

She looked up at the tree again, turning from him. "No

tree usually."

"I wonder what's more pathetic. No tree or a bunch of trees that no one really appreciated."

She shot him a glance. "That's a tough call. I bought a fake tree for Dani the first year she came to live with me. I thought it would cheer her up."

"Did it?"

She nodded. "Yup, a bit. I know she was happy that she was living with me, but I think at that age it's still hard to leave a parent, no matter how negligent they were."

He looked down at the ground for a moment. "How is your mom doing?"

She took off a glove and ran her bare fingers across a few branches. "The same. She's one of those people who just can't get it together, you know? She's not a bad person, but she probably shouldn't have had kids." She said the last part softly and it made him think about things he wasn't used to. She made him feel things he wasn't used to. Allie brought out this soft side of him, the side that he could never show his family. Here, with her, it made him think that maybe he had what she needed. White snow clung to her brown hair, and her admission hung in the air.

Hell, he wanted to identify with her. He wanted to tell her about himself, but he hadn't talked about those days in years. He didn't like being soft or reminded of a time when he was so weak and at the mercy of others. But the look in her eyes when they'd been in his office still haunted him. She'd be a woman he could tell his secrets to. In her own way she'd understand him. If he ever let someone in it would be Allie. It wasn't only his secrets, his past. He wanted to know about hers. He wished he could be the guy to make it all better, to make promises.

She walked away from him for a moment and dropped her coffee cup into the bin and then joined him again. "What about your parents? You do anything special for Christmas?"

He shrugged. "We meet for brunch Christmas morning."

"Oh…that sounds…nice."

He grinned. "It's hell, actually. My brother sits there trying to impress our father, my brother's wife or girlfriend of the day spends the entire time admiring whatever piece of jewelry his secretary bought her, and we all open gifts that none of us even picked out ourselves."

Her mouth dropped open. "What do you mean?"

"Ann, my assistant, buys a present for my father, mother, and brother."

"Ethan!"

He laughed. "It's a family tradition. Hand over a credit card and you're done."

"That's kind of sad."

"We're not a close family."

She put her glove back on, not looking at him. "Funny, I always thought you came from this great family. Sometimes it's so easy to assume that when you have money things are so much better."

"Well, we don't have to worry about food or where to live, so in that respect it's better."

"Did you ever imagine yourself with your own family? Having your own traditions?"

He took a step closer to her and then stopped himself. What the hell was he doing? No, he didn't think of his own family. He didn't think of kids. But he thought of her. And maybe in some crazy place inside, where he let himself imagine such things, he'd think of Allie being his wife. A mother. She was staring at him, her gaze locked on his. Even he wasn't immune to the moment, the scent of cedar enveloping them, the gentle snowfall, the fresh country air. Damn, what was happening to him?

She must have assumed he wasn't going to say a thing

because she started speaking. "I never thought of that kind of stuff. You know that crap line that little girls sit there imagining their wedding? Not me. I had bigger stuff to worry about. But when Hannah and Jackson got married…that little church in the country…"

Her voice trailed off and she looked beyond him, a slight sheen in her eyes.

"Yeah," he said, his voice sounding hoarse. "Those two make it look easy."

She looked down at her boots. "He's a good guy."

Hell. Jackson was a good guy, but it still made him feel jealous, because he wanted to be one of those good guys. He wanted Allie. He wanted for the first time in his life to have a meaningful relationship. He wanted a woman for more than a night. Not any woman, Allie. Only Allie.

He nodded. "He is." He walked over to where she was, telling himself he was just going to brush the snow off her hair, because they couldn't be anything more. He wasn't good enough for her, and he would hurt her. But that didn't stop him from walking over to her.

"Allie, is that you?"

He whipped his head around as some lumberjack type guy came running over. Allie let out some kind of squeal and ran—*jumped*—into the guy's waiting arms. Mr. Blueberry. Ethan stood there as jealousy beat through his body in a mocking rhythm. What he wanted to do was walk over and rip that man's hands off Allie. He checked a temper he wasn't aware he had and mentally counted down.

"It's so great to see you, Sam," Allie said in that sweet voice of hers.

He smiled down at her with what Ethan thought were very dopey looking eyes. He would assume that some women would find his outdoorsy looks appealing. "Great to see you, too, honey."

Time to insert himself. It was the honey endearment. When he stepped next to Allie and grabbed her hand, she looked up at him. The shocked look in her eyes was either due to the fact that she had forgotten he was even here, or that he was holding her hand. "Oh, Ethan, this is my…good friend, Sam Cromwell."

Sam Cromwell held out his hand. Ethan shook it, pissed at what a firm handshake it was.

"Nice to meet you, Ethan."

"Likewise," Ethan said. "This is your farm?"

Sam nodded. "Yep."

"So, you're into blueberries?"

Sam stood a little straighter like he was on to the fact that Ethan thought he was an idiot. "My grandparents started the farm. They named it."

Ethan nodded. "How do you two know each other?"

Sam's lips parted like a giant whale. "We go way back."

Allie looked up at Ethan. "We dated for a while."

"Best few weeks of my life," Sam said, leaning against one of the trees.

He hoped it would fall over. "Great. So, we're here for a tree," Ethan said. He pointed to the tree Allie had already shown him. "I think Allie wants that one. How much do we owe you?"

"For Allie? It's on the house."

Ethan took out his wallet. "I insist."

"Sam, that's so sweet of you, but I'm paying."

"I've got it," Ethan said, baring his teeth like a Neanderthal.

"No, it's on the house," Sam said, standing a little straighter. Dammit if they weren't the same height.

"Guys," Allie said in some primary school teacher's voice. "I'm paying. It's going down as an expense for the shelter."

Sam held up his hands. "I'll take it to your car."

"I'll take it," Ethan said.

"Company policy. I'll take it."

Ethan shrugged and watched him lift the tree effortlessly. "Fine. I'd hate to go against official Blueberry Hill policy. We'll be there in a minute." Once he was out of earshot, Ethan turned to look at Allie. She was currently scowling at him.

Her foot was tapping against the snow-covered ground, making a crunching noise whenever it hit the snow. "What was that all about?"

"So he's the ex?"

She crossed her arms and tucked her hat down lower over her forehead, but not low enough to cover her scowl. "Yes."

"Why'd you break up? Tell me it was you who broke up with him."

"I find your attitude very disturbing, as is your barking out all these questions. I refuse to answer you unless you back down."

Ethan held up his hands. "Back down? I'm not being confrontational. I'm just curious."

"We broke up because he couldn't give me what I needed."

Ethan couldn't stop the grin from spreading on his face.

She swatted him with her mitten. "It wasn't him. It was me. I wanted that all-encompassing love, that desire that makes a person shake. The weak in the knees thing."

"I could have told you he wouldn't have given that to you. I could have spared you weeks of your life."

Her mouth dropped open. "You're acting insane."

"No, Allie. I'm acting like a guy who has asked you out three times and had you refuse me. I'm acting like said guy who then has to meet some blueberry farmer that you *did* agree to date. I will also tell you that Weekend Ethan is arriving tomorrow and—"

Her squeal of outrage interrupted him. "What did you just say?"

He couldn't help but smile, even though she was royally

pissed, hands on her hips, with a look that told him she was ready to kick his ass. "Yeah, Weekend Ethan. You know, with scruff so appealing you want to lick my face."

She yelled as she lunged for him. He managed to duck as she tried to hit him, but he was laughing so hard she managed to get him in the shoulder. "I can't believe you! I wasn't dreaming. You're awful!"

Her face was bright red, and he managed to grab her hand, tugging her over to him. "I don't think you really think I'm awful."

"Do *not* quote me again."

"Fine. I don't need to quote you. Yes, last night was very, very real, and I haven't stopped thinking about you since. I'll tell you what I know. That chemistry you wanted with Spam the blueberry farmer? We have it. You'll know that when I kiss you in less than one minute from now."

"Uh, you wish, and his name is Sam."

"Your world will stop. Your knees will be so weak you'll have to hold on to me. You'll forget where you are, who you are, and everything except wanting more."

Her mouth dropped open, and a little sound that sent blood pumping through his veins came out of her mouth. Ethan stepped into her space and cupped her face, every muscle tightly wound in his body. Snow fell around them, and they were isolated amidst the rows and rows of trees on the hill. She didn't move; her eyes were on his and he knew, could feel the desire running through her.

"What are you doing?" she whispered, her gaze going from his eyes to his lips.

"I'm showing you what it's like to forget where you are, who you are, and everything except wanting more." He dipped his head and finally tasted the woman that kept him up at night, thinking, wanting. But he wasn't going to rush this. He was going to savor every second, and he was going to show her exactly how good they could be together. He softly brushed his lips against one corner of her mouth, and she sighed. Her hands clutched his forearms when he said her name against her lips and then sank his hands into her hair.

That was the end of taking it slow. He kissed her wet and deep, and Allie tasted better than he remembered. She tasted of cinnamon and vanilla…and Allie. And he couldn't get enough. He fisted his hands in her hair, pulling her closer, kissing her until he was pretty damn sure he made good on every one of his arrogant promises. Her hands went from his forearms to his chest and tugged on the lapels of his coat, pulling him closer, until he was drowning in Allie.

"Your tree is ready!" a voice called out, sounding like Spam.

"Wow," she whispered, still clutching his forearms and moving back slightly.

"We could have had this for three years if you'd said yes."

She looked up at him, her eyes filled with something that looked like insecurity. She let go of his arms and took a step back. "Three years ago I had a hard time picturing you as anything but a guy looking for a good time and no strings."

"Sweetie, if they were your strings, I wouldn't have had a problem."

She almost gave him a smile. "Ethan…I don't…I've been on my own for a long time and things run well. I don't like relying on people because they always fail me, even though so far you haven't." She paused to sweep her arm in some sort of circular motion around him. "You've come through for me." Her brow furrowed, and he tried to keep calm even though he felt like crap, because he wasn't going to come through for her in the end. In the end, he'd end up hurting her. He shouldn't have started any of this, but when he looked down at her, blue eyes staring into his with vulnerability and trust… it killed him. He couldn't walk away from her.

"Ethan, you are so much more than I expected, but my life is a shit-show most days. I have a mother that requires more help than a child, a dependent attitude-filled teenage sister, and a disabled dog. I was raised in low-income housing, never met my dad, and did groceries regularly at the food bank. These designer clothes I'm wearing are the first I've ever owned, and they're because of you. I'm not telling you this so that you can feel bad for me. I'm grateful to you, more than I'll ever be able to tell you — and I will pay you back, with interest."

He cleared his throat because it was filled with emotion. Everything she'd just said made him want to tell his family to go to hell and just spend the rest of his life with Allie. He was turning into Jackson. "Allie, there is no way in hell—"

"But I don't want any of this permanently. This is not me. I like simple things. I don't like keeping up appearances."

He shrugged. "I couldn't give a rat's ass about appearances."

"I want *real*, Ethan."

"Then I guess I'll have to show you real again," he said, lifting his hands to cup her face. Her skin was soft and her breath hitched as he made contact with her.

"Seriously, I'm not joking. Do not kiss me again until I finish what I'm saying."

"Go ahead, you were saying something about needing real."

"Right," she said, licking her lips quickly and looking at his mouth. He fought his urge to smile.

"Maybe you got me all wrong. Maybe you just don't know enough about me." He ran his thumb along her cheekbone, wanting to convince her that he was more than who she thought. "I like your sister and Hook. As for your mother, who am I to judge? You should meet my family."

She gave him a small smile. "I get that, but it's not what I mean…you and I would never work."

"You think I'm shallow."

She shook her head then nodded. He laughed and tried not to take it too personally.

"I don't, Ethan. Sometimes I get this hint of someone else, like that day you kicked me out of your office. I've known you for three years, and I've been living at your place for almost two weeks, but I still don't feel like I *know* you. I don't know anything more about you than I did when we first met. I get that you didn't want me in your office for whatever reason, but I think your reaction was still…weird."

He winced and then pulled her into his arms. He was surprised when he felt her arms wrap around his waist. He didn't want to tell her, he didn't want her sympathy, or even worse, he didn't want to be seen as someone weak. She felt she didn't know him, but he didn't know how to be any more real without delving into a part of himself that he didn't feel comfortable with. He didn't like that Ethan.

He liked the Ethan who kicked ass at work, who kicked ass at the gym, and was in control of his life. He didn't like thinking of the kid who had no control over anything. "I'm sorry about that, sweetie," he said against the top of her head. Allie smelled like the outdoors and some kind of flowery shampoo. He was sorry he'd hurt her that day, and he was sorry he couldn't let her in. What the hell was he supposed to do now? She was basically telling him that she thought he was hollow. So his choices were to let Allie go and keep all his shit safely inside, or open up to her and…

"I know, but you still didn't tell me…there are things that I saw." He pulled back, taking a step away. Her eyes were on him, sharp. "We should probably get back to the shelter or it'll be too late to trim the tree."

"You're right. Let's see if Spam was able to get the tree on top of my SUV."

"Sam. His name is Sam."

Chapter Eight

An hour later, Allie was standing on the street corner watching Ethan lug the tree into the shelter. He was refusing to let her help, so she held the door open for him. Denise rushed over, as did a few of the kids to watch him.

She smiled as Max decided to join Ethan and help bring the tree into the main room.

"Thanks, man," Ethan said as Max held the tree while he assembled the base he'd purchased on their way there. Allie tried to focus on the conversation with the group that surrounded them, and not on how hot Ethan looked taking charge of everything. This was stuff she always had to do. He'd stepped in and done everything with ease. Spending the day with him, just the two of them had been…nice as well as revealing.

He had been jealous of Sam. She'd hoped he would have opened up to her and maybe let her in. Instead, he'd proven the whole crazy attraction thing she'd been after. He'd made her forget everything. She had never been kissed like that— well, she had the night before. Now she knew she hadn't been dreaming, and apparently she'd told the man she wanted to lick his face. That was the last time she was drinking by herself.

Today he'd taken over, kissed her like he wanted her, with a passion that was all consuming, but when she questioned him, he'd shut her down. He tossed his coat on one of the armchairs and was now securing the tree with Max while another one of the boys held the tree in position. She should have been pulling the boxes of decorations over, not checking out him or the muscles that seemed to take his Henley to a whole new level.

She shouldn't be thinking about any of that. She should be remembering that Ethan was emotionally unavailable. So, great, the one guy who managed to rock her world with just a kiss was closed off emotionally. "Wipe up your drool, Missy," Denise whispered in her ear.

Allie covered her face. "It's so true, I am drooling."

"With good cause. I just hope you don't mess this up."

Allie frowned at her friend. "Thanks for the vote of confidence."

Denise put her arm around her shoulder. "I mean, when you guys get close, or he wants to get close, you shut down and come up with five thousand excuses as to why you'd never work."

"I really hate that you know so much about me," she whispered, still watching Ethan interact with the kids as he secured the tree. She and Denise had bonded almost instantly and after putting in long nights and days together, they had both opened up about their pasts. She knew just as much about her friend.

"Allie, what do you think?"

Ethan's deep voice rang out across the room, and she guiltily whipped her gaze away from his chest to his eyes. He was standing by the tree, asking her if it was in the right position. He was looking so delicious and sweet and sexy…

she cleared her throat and nodded rapidly. "Perfect. Let's start stringing the lights."

Denise rummaged through a box and then handed her a giant ball of tangled lights. "Good luck keeping your eyes on the lights," she whispered.

Ethan walked over to them and held his hand out. "I'll get this done in five minutes."

Allie tried not to laugh. "Have you ever done this?"

He took the lights. "It's a bunch of lights. Big deal."

Half an hour later, Allie reminded Ethan for the tenth time not to swear out loud. The kids seemed to think it was hilarious. Hot chocolate was being passed around, and they were helping unpack the decorations. Ethan seemed to be making progress, despite his vocal frustration.

"Huh. I think we're going on thirty-five minutes now. Seems like half an hour longer than—"

"Done," he said triumphantly, standing with the lights completely unraveled. Everyone clapped and whistled.

He held up his hands, smiling. The man had just successfully charmed and won over a room full of teenagers, her, and Denise. "Thanks. Who knows how to string these?"

"Allie does," one of the girls called out.

"Yup. I'm the expert." She held out her hands for the first string of lights and started walking to the ladder. "Also, I know enough not to put a ridiculous timeline on such things." She gave Ethan a smirk just as she walked into the ladder. He quickly held it still for her. It was that damn smile of his that was all distracting.

"Denise, I think we need Christmas music," she said as she climbed the ladder to the top. She looked down and caught Ethan staring at her in that way that made her body feel like it was a furnace about to explode, because his eyes weren't on hers, not right away. They roamed lazily up her body until they reached her eyes. By that time she was regretting wearing a wool sweater. She should have been dressed for the tropics.

"Don't fall," he said, handing her the first string of lights with one hand and lightly holding on to her hip with the other.

"Thanks for the advice," she said, trying to concentrate on getting the lights tightly wrapped around the top branches and not the feel of his hand on her body.

Ethan stood in the cramped room drinking coffee and admiring Allie as she mingled with the teens. Everyone loved her; it was obvious in the ease with which most of them addressed her, the casual rapport she had with them. She laughed, she teased, and she spoke gently to the more distant ones.

He looked around, taking in the space. It had actually been a fun night. The kids were now filtering out and the room was almost empty. Allie and Denise were in the dining room and he'd told her he'd wait here for her. The Christmas tree cast a warm glow to the room and it did truly feel like a home, even though it was shelter for kids who didn't have a home. But all the youth workers and support staff made it feel real. Feeling…something she accused him of being unable to. Was he incapable of feeling? Of course not. Yet, he was lacking in that department according to Allie.

He glanced over at her. Her brown hair was piled slightly crazily atop her head, held together with a big clip. Her red sweater clung to the curves he found himself admiring every day. Her smile was gorgeous, and her eyes twinkled as she laughed with a few girls. So, see, he felt things. He felt lots of things, besides the obvious.

Ethan sat down on the couch that was now empty and contemplated this lack of feeling comment while he waited for Allie. A kid sat on an armchair opposite him, propping his feet on the coffee table. He was the same teen he'd seen that first night he'd picked Allie up.

Ethan stared at the kid's sour expression. He knew that expression—it was the universal closed-off, mutinous face worn by every teenager at some point in time. He knew this kid probably thought he couldn't relate to him, and hell, he couldn't in a lot of ways, except one.

"You like it here?"

Max shrugged, hunkered farther down into the cushions, and settled into a scowl. Allie happened to walk by at that moment, and Ethan watched as the kid's gaze trailed her appreciatively.

"You like her?"

Max jerked his head toward him, a funny red creeping up his neck. "She's cool."

"She is."

"She your girlfriend?"

Ethan paused. "No. Just a good friend."

"So you're an idiot."

He bit back a laugh and stretched out his legs. The couch wasn't exactly comfortable but it was clean. "Sometimes people don't want to ruin a good thing, so they don't move forward."

Max bent his head and pretended to study whatever it was in his notebook. "Don't you have anything better to do on Saturday? You look like you're somebody important."

Ethan shrugged. "I'm waiting for Allie to finish up. I wanted to come here tonight."

"What do you do?"

"I own a tech company."

"Really? That sounds cool."

He nodded. "It is pretty cool." See? He could relate to people. He could feel things. Right now he felt genuine concern for these kids and this kid in particular.

"I bet you need a lot of money to start up a company."

Ethan sat up. "Not really, but it doesn't hurt. My buddy didn't have any money. He got a full scholarship to one of the best schools in the country. When we graduated we started up."

"Yeah, but I bet you bankrolled it." There was an edge in his voice, like he'd already decided he couldn't do something like that.

"No, he wouldn't let me because he didn't want to be indebted to me. We started out of a basement apartment. We made some lucky connections and got a few lucky breaks, but we worked our asses off and took a lot of risks. Anyone can do that."

Max shrugged, his expression closing up again and hiding the spark of interest Ethan had spotted.

"Yeah, well, it's stupid to waste my time dreaming about shit that will never happen. I'd never get into a school like that. I fucked up my first two years of high school."

"That doesn't matter. Fix it now."

Max rubbed his head with a frustrated sigh. "I'm trying."

"This seems like a place that can help you."

"It is."

"It's not too late. You're like, what, fifteen?"

"Sixteen." He said it like it was the equivalent to eighty.

"So get your ass in gear and get your grades up."

Max grabbed his books in a huff, and Ethan felt bad for being so blunt with him. "Hey, man, I was just trying to offer you some advice."

"Yeah, well, the last thing I need is advice from some rich prick who thinks he's doing Good Samaritan work and impressing some chick he wants to bang. Save it for someone who actually gives a shit."

He watched his first attempt at motivating a troubled teen storm out of the room. He let out a deep breath. Shit. He thought Dani was a lot to handle. How the hell did Allie do this all day?

He glanced down at his watch. She should be finished anytime now. He stood and walked over to the Christmas tree. It was nice. Everyone had done a good job. Nothing fancy but it made the main gathering room seem festive. He wondered how many of these kids had had one of these growing up. He'd had one in every single room of his childhood home. They were all grand. They all had a different color scheme depending on the room's decor, and they all reached the twelve-foot ceilings yet not a damn one evoked the warmth this one did.

Guilt danced around his mind as he thought of that Max kid. He heard soft voices in the hallway and after a few seconds of listening he recognized them as Allie and Max. He looked in the direction of the door and saw Max give her a smile—it was a half-smile and then he looked down. Allie was smiling back at him and emotion hit him in the gut, rendering him incapable of moving. She had this light about her, a glow, an inherent goodness that begged and screamed at the best pieces of him to come forward. It made him want to forget all the reasons he couldn't have Allie, the foremost being that he wasn't good enough for a woman like that. He would hurt her, and he would disappoint her, and seeing disappointment from her would kill him. But knowing her even better than before was making it impossible for him to stay away. For once in his life he wanted the good, he wanted to surround himself with people that forced him to be better, to be bigger than the small world he lived in.

Allie reminded him of Nurse Annie. Annie had been like a mother to him, and sometimes when he'd be sick and scared and lying in that hospital bed at night, he'd make silly little wishes and would ask God to make Annie his mom. He knew that it couldn't possibly happen, of course, but Annie would hold him like she knew he needed someone to hold on to him, because he'd be scared he would disappear and be taken from the world when he shut his eyes. Annie made him believe he would always be here.

It was Annie who had held on to him when he cried for Cara. It was Annie who cheered the loudest when he'd been given the all clear. It was Annie who he had run to with the biggest of hugs. And he'd never held on to another person like that again. Annie taught him how to love and somewhere along the way he'd forgotten. He'd forgotten about that special feeling.

He blinked back the moisture in his eyes and focused on the little gold angel on the tree. He still thought of Annie, fleeting thoughts, and he'd quickly bury them. But this time of year brought out all those memories. He had never ventured back there, never went to see Annie again even though he promised he would. He made his donations, the largest donations he made anywhere, and he had gifts sent to the kids every year, but he never went back. In days he'd be forced to revisit the part of his past no one knew about. It was like his own little personal hell that rose up and attempted to choke him once a year.

"I'm all ready to go." Allie's voice sweetly brought him back to where he was now, and he turned to her. He didn't move for a moment, finding it hard to transition out of his reflective state and deal with a present that didn't allow him to be real and open. Allie would hold someone like that. She'd hold on and will her strength and goodness into the other person.

"Ethan? You okay?"

He nodded, finding his voice, reminding himself of why it was better not to think of crap like this. Feeling was highly overrated. "Great." He walked across the room to grab his coat and shrugged into it.

"You okay? You look a little less like you're ready to conquer the world."

He smiled, taking in the hat and scarf. She was gorgeous at the end of a long day, bundled up for winter. She was the most beautiful woman he'd ever known, inside and out. And selfish bastard that he was, he wanted a part of it.

He grabbed her hand, and she followed along. He needed to get outside, to have her to himself, before he remembered all the reasons he couldn't have her, before he remembered he was going to break her heart and the heart of everyone in this place. A gush of cold air and tumbling snow greeted them as they emerged from the warm shelter.

"Don't kill me for saying it, but I'm so happy it's snowing." Allie laughed, and just like every other time she laughed, he felt that happiness creep in. He looked down at her and stood there for half a second before stepping into her and threading his fingers through her hair. Her mouth dropped open, and he read the surprise in those gorgeous eyes of hers.

The desire and excitement, the welcome of his touch, that was all he needed before lowering his mouth to hers. Allie tasted of candy canes and sweetness. She wrapped her arms around him and kissed him back and he forgot about where they were standing. All he could think about was feeling the present, the moment, the woman.

Chapter Nine

Ethan held the door to his condo open for her, and Allie slipped past him. She was still reeling from their day, from his kisses, and from the man himself. The kiss at the farm had—as promised—rocked her world completely. She'd already known they had chemistry, and she had been ignoring that chemistry for years. What she hadn't counted on was that she'd feel something more than just chemistry from his kiss. Or that he'd feel more. Not that she could attest for what the man felt, but the entire thing had felt real.

Then there was the whole thing at Haven House. The tree decorating, his natural charm that had won over even the surliest of the teens—even Max looked somewhat intrigued by Ethan. He had hung around and socialized and helped as though it was the best thing he could be doing on a Saturday night. Then he'd kissed her outside with a passion or a need that was palpable.

There was something in his eyes, though, as she replayed the night, when she'd gone in to find him standing next to the Christmas tree. Ethan had looked vulnerable, and he never looked vulnerable. Boyish, yes, but not actually vulnerable. It had been in the way he'd stood there, hands in his pockets, the tilt of that firm chin, the glint in his eyes. Whatever it was that he was keeping inside, a part of her was concerned. It made her think of the picture in his office, the books, the D-Day on his calendar.

"You totally rocked the tree-trimming event. And if I had some kind of access to ribbons or medals or gold stars, I would totally give you one, because there is no way I could have pulled that off by myself."

His grin was infectious, partly because it had that whole boyish thing she'd just been thinking about, and partly because he was walking closer to her. It was as though their kiss had demolished whatever barrier they'd had up before. He'd dropped his jacket on the chair at the front and was wearing the Henley and his worn jeans. She'd expected him to always look designer, and maybe it was because she knew he came from money and was usually dressed in designer suits for work, but at home he looked casual. Not preppy. He wore his clothes the way he did everything, with a confidence and casual grace that she admired. She loved "Weekend Ethan" who didn't shave and wore a ratty baseball cap. She admired him in a lot of ways when she wasn't busy salivating over him, like she was now, because he was standing in front of her, the boyishness gone as he stared into her eyes.

"I don't need a medal."

She tapped her finger on her chin. "Gold star."

He grinned, wide and gorgeous and downright sexy as he leaned close to her. His mouth was a few inches from hers, and it took all the self-control she had not to reach up and kiss him. "Spend the night with me, Allie."

Her heart stopped for a second, and a rush of blood tore through her. She forced a calm expression on her face. "I think that reward is a little disproportionate for the task."

He laughed, low and deep, and set off another avalanche of feelings through her body. "I meant, like, have a glass of wine with me and talk."

She cleared her throat and refused to look embarrassed, if that were possible. "Oh. Oh, of course that's what you meant. Sure, I'd love a glass of wine."

He grinned again and grabbed her hand, then they walked to the kitchen. "Are you hungry?"

She could eat anything and everything she was so hungry. Then she remembered the cookie debacle at the farm. "A little."

Ethan opened the fridge then shut it a second later. "How about takeout?"

Considering the man only ate health food she was hesitant to agree. "What do you usually order?" She really needed comfort food, not salad and protein.

"I don't usually order. I usually go out or cook something." He leaned casually against the granite counter. He looked good enough to eat. She purposely took a step back. She never should have let that kiss happen, or the second one. It was much easier to keep at a distance before. Now she had to contend with this insane urge to jump him.

"Do you like Thai food?"

He nodded. "Sure. How about I order while you get us set up in the other room?"

"Great. I'll get wine."

"Help yourself to anything. Maybe avoid the rum. I'll have a glass of red," he said, scrolling through his phone.

"It's rude of you to mention the rum mishap."

"Is that how we're referring to it now?"

"That was the end of referring to it at all."

Seconds later she heard him placing an order. She walked across the large space and turned on one of the table lamps. It cast a warm glow to the dark space. The rest of the lighting was taken care of by the city skyline.

Ethan walked in a second later. "Food is on its way."

"Seriously? The one night Ethan orders delivery and I'm not going to be here?" Dani stood in the doorway with a backpack on her shoulder and a frown on her face.

She crossed her arms and eyed her sister. "Where are you going to be?"

Dani sighed theatrically and let her bag drop to the floor. "Sandra's."

Ethan poured wine into two glasses, not saying anything.

"Be home by—"

"I'm sleeping there."

Allie accepted the glass of wine Ethan handed her. It was perfect timing. She knew Sandra was one of Dani's best friends. She just needed to be sure that Dani was telling the truth.

"You need to tell me—*ask* me actually—instead of just telling me. Also, I need to speak with her mom." Allie took a long sip of her wine as Dani let out a screech of what she presumed was mortification.

She stomped her foot. "You are not calling!"

Ethan held out his phone in her direction.

"Thank you, Ethan. Phone number, Dani." She gave her sister a pointed look and waited.

"Oh my God, I'm dying right now."

Ethan turned to her, obviously holding in his grin. "Call 911, then call the friend's mom."

Dani flopped onto the couch. "Ugh. What could I have possibly done to earn this lack of trust?"

Ethan coughed. "Uh, I can think of a time, not that long ago actually…"

Allie turned from the conversation and spoke with Sandra's mother. "Fine, all clear," she said a moment later. She placed Ethan's phone on the end table. "I confirmed with her mom. She also said that you are both staying in tonight, right?"

Dani rolled her eyes and nodded.

"How are you getting there?" Ethan asked.

Dani's face lit up like a Christmas tree. "Are you offering me one of your cars?"

He took out his wallet. "I'm offering you money for a cab."

"Put your wallet away," Allie said, attempting to snatch it. Instead, she almost spilled her wine all over the man.

Dani made some sort of theatrical sigh. "Allie, don't be such a downer all the time."

Ethan handed her sister some money and minutes later she was leaving.

"You don't have to do that, you know." Allie had to admit it was a nice feeling, though, having another adult in the room. Her sister was a force to be reckoned with, and she was always by herself. He'd come through for her. Again.

Ethan watched Allie from across the room, sipping her wine. He thought of what Dani had said about their mom. They had finished eating dinner and had cleared the dishes and were now back in the living room. He had never realized how alone he had been, how empty this space had felt without Allie.

"Thanks again for putting up with Dani's antics."

He shrugged and sat down beside her on the couch. He needed to tell her about the night she'd passed out on his bed. "I've got to tell you something."

The way she leaned forward, concern making her eyes deepen, touched him. He knew she thought he was going to open up to her. He ran his hands through his hair. "The night you…came on to me when you were in my bed?"

"I don't recall a night like this," she said, looking into her glass.

"Dani called your cell phone. I picked it up. She was stuck at some party with some loser guy that ditched her."

She put down the rest of her wine and smacked her hands over her mouth.

"So I went to pick her up—she was fine. Nothing bad happened. I lectured her the entire way home. She begged me not to tell you…" His voice trailed off when her eyes filled with tears. "I expected you to be pissed with me for not telling you."

"You went and picked up my sister. You made her wrap presents. She even said she loved me."

He swallowed hard and then nodded.

"Thank you," she whispered into her glass of wine. "You have no idea what that means to me. I've been on my own for so long, and I never rely on anyone. You came through for me, Ethan. You took us in, no questions asked, after the fire. You gave us food and clothes, you totally helped with the shelter…and Dani…" She stopped speaking and looked up at the ceiling. "I have never had someone to rely on, and you came through for me." She looked back at him, bringing with her gaze every ounce of feeling and emotion that had been missing from his life. He needed her not to think of him like that, because he would destroy all her trust if she only knew. He should come up with some kind of excuse and walk away from her. He'd wanted her from the moment he first saw her, and now she was here, in his home, and staring at him with the most gorgeous mix of desire and trust. If he were a better man, that's what he'd do.

He was filled with his own demons, his own fucked-up problems he didn't want to bother her with. D-Day was next week, and if there were a problem, he'd never let her know.

He'd just walk away. Maybe this was his last chance to be with her before his entire life went to hell, and if it wasn't, he'd find a way to make it right for her.

"In the car Dani said something about your mom needing money?"

Her mouth dropped open and she looked away. "What else did she say?"

"Not much. She was sorry about yelling at you, and I think she feels like your mom takes advantage of you."

She shrugged and avoided eye contact. Then she picked at her jeans.

"Allie…"

"You would never understand."

"Try me."

She raised an eyebrow. "It's not a unique story. Single parent family. No dad that I know of. Dani and I have different fathers, but hers is MIA, too. My mother tried her best, but she's an alcoholic. She almost lost me, but got sober in order to keep me. That's how I first learned the serenity prayer."

His muscles felt tight, and he wanted to acknowledge the prayer, what she was trying to do by showing them their connection, but he couldn't do that. He didn't want to acknowledge that part. He wanted to ask a thousand questions, but he knew he had to play it cool; he didn't want her to back away. "So what happened with Dani? Why did you take her in?"

She took a noticeably tiny sip of wine. "Because she started drinking again. Sometimes I feel bad because I didn't notice right away."

"It's pretty amazing you did that."

"Family. She's my little sister, and there was no way I was going to leave her there."

"And how's your mom now?"

She ran a hand through her hair. "Not great. She's been

with the same guy now for years, so I guess that's good. Except they both drink, and they have trouble making rent."

"And that's why she needed money from you?"

She nodded, and he put his hand on her thigh. "I, uh, I feel indebted to her, for something that happened a long time ago," she said in a low voice, breaking his stare.

He forced himself to look calm even though, thanks to Dani, he already knew where this was headed. "What happened, sweetheart?"

She blinked a few times, staring into the fire. "One of her boyfriends started coming into my room when I was twelve." She stopped talking, and he stopped breathing. He hoped to hell this story wasn't going to go there, that she didn't have to endure what he thought was coming next. He didn't know how he'd handle it, how he'd keep it all together. Just the idea of someone hurting Allie intentionally, especially the child version of Allie, was too much.

"At first it was little things. Hugs. Then the hugs lasted a little longer. And I would tell my mom because I was scared. I was totally grossed out. I can still remember his smell. He smelled like beer and BO."

Ethan wanted to kill someone. Him. That perverted asshole. He wanted to hunt him down and kill him. "What happened?" he managed to ask, not even recognizing his voice.

Allie downed the rest of her wine and set it on the coffee table. He looked at the empty glass, remembering what Dani had said about Allie drinking.

"Things progressed a little…but the night he tried to… and wanted me to do things to him, my mom caught him, and she got rid of him. She believed me."

Ethan stared at her wondering how the hell Allie had turned out so good. How all this had happened to her and she didn't walk around scarred. How she could expect so little of her mother, almost as though what her mother had done was above and beyond.

"Your mother chose you, her daughter, and that's the way it should be. Her believing you should have been a given," he whispered.

"For her it wasn't. For many it isn't." She looked at him, this time with a plea in her eyes, her gorgeous mouth trembling. "I don't want to talk about this. I want to be doing anything but talking about this."

He leaned forward, cupping the back of her head, his gaze going from her eyes to her lips. "Thank you for telling me."

"I trust you, Ethan," she said. He knew that he hadn't told her about his past. But tonight wasn't about him. It was about her. It was about Allie trusting him, feeling safe with him. He was humbled, and he was falling. He leaned closer, wanting her more than anyone else, ever. She met him halfway. She leaned into him, and he took her mouth in his. Allie moaned sweetly as he moved to cover her body, leaning back into the couch. He kissed her until he couldn't remember his own name, until neither of them could think about anything other than being with each other. She kissed him back with every ounce of desire, every emotion. He slid his hand under her sweater, cupping a soft, perfect breast, while the other roamed up her thigh to palm her sweet ass. Her soft, curvy body pressed up against his, and he dragged his mouth from her lips to her earlobe. She had her hands in his hair.

"God, I want you, Allie. Right from the first night. I knew we'd be like this together," he whispered in between trailing kisses from her neck back up to her mouth.

A pounding on the door jolted them. He ignored it and kissed her again. Until the pounding started again. He cursed softly. They were both breathing raggedly, and he lowered his forehead to hers. "I'm going to kill whoever is on the other side of that door."

"Who is it?" she whispered.

"Whoever it is, they are no friend of mine," he said. But the knocking continued, and by the sounds of it, it was probably one of his friends. He disengaged his limbs from the best thing that ever happened to him and stood. He ran his hands through his hair and looked down at Allie. She was trying to smooth out her hair and looked completely irresistible. He leaned down to kiss her one last time before dragging himself away and walking to the front door.

He swung it open and stared at Nicholas Wright's grim face. "What the hell? Don't you have anything else better to do on a Saturday night?"

His friend looked at him up and down. "I don't, but apparently you do."

Allie appeared in the hallway, and Ethan decided it was time to compartmentalize Nick. There was only one reason his friend was here, and there was no way he wanted Allie to know anything about it. "Uh, Allie, this is my friend Nicholas Wright."

Nicholas gave him a look that was unmistakably apologetic. "Nice to meet you, Allie," he said, shaking her hand.

"Nick, go wait for me in my office," Ethan said.

Nicholas gave him a small salute and walked down the hall.

Ethan walked up to Allie, who had her arms folded across her chest. "So, what's this all about?"

"I'm sorry, sweetheart. We had some unfinished contracts to go over, but I had no idea he'd be coming over tonight." He was so screwed, and he was a bigger jerk than even before. He didn't want to leave her alone, especially after everything she'd just told him. He wanted her in his arms, in his bed, he wanted to make love to her and make her feel loved and safe. But instead he was going to go over plans to move forward with closing down her shelter.

She gave a little nod. "So *he's* allowed in your office?"

Shit. "He's different, he's a guy. He doesn't look at things. He sits down and starts talking contracts."

She poked him in the stomach, and he grabbed her hand, tugging her into him for a long kiss. The door crashed open and they both jumped. Dani was standing there looking royally pissed. "I no longer have a BFF. Sandra is dead to me."

So much for a night of just the two of them.

Chapter Ten

Allie huddled farther into her coat and hopped from one foot to the other. It was almost five o'clock on Monday, and she was standing outside a large office building. It was rush hour, and the streets and sidewalks were packed.

She was huddled in the alcove so she wasn't in anyone's way. She had waited inside forever, but there was no sign of Ethan. She knew what today was, and she was almost in semi-panic mode. Normally she would have taken in the pretty cityscape at Christmas time. Nearby businesses all had twinkling lights and greenery, the air smelled of exhaust… and of cinnamon…huh. She spotted the bakery on the street corner and promised herself that if he didn't emerge from the building in half an hour, she'd get herself the most ginormous cinnamon bun money could buy.

After Saturday night's interrupted…whatever, Ethan had changed. His entire mood had shifted, and he was distant and preoccupied. Sunday morning he went out for his usual run, but this time when he came back home he just claimed he had a lot of work and spent most of the day in his office.

Allie first thought it had something to do with his lawyer's visit, but then she remembered that today was the infamous/mysterious D-Day on his calendar. She'd woken up extra early to try and have a moment with him, but he'd already been gone. She called his office from work at least half a dozen times, but was always told he was unavailable. She then decided she'd have to finagle some kind of information out of his receptionist Ann. Ann was notorious for being private, but after a quick call to Hannah, Allie found out some news: apparently, Ethan was inside the building at some kind of medical appointment. As soon as Allie finished up at the shelter she'd jumped on a streetcar to this address and had been waiting ever since.

She glanced down at her watch and groaned. She was freezing, and he was nowhere in sight. She had texted him five times, and he normally always texted her back within minutes. Today? Silence. After five more minutes, she decided she'd pop into the bakery, grab her cinnamon bun, and then run back to her perch. And then when she saw Ethan, she'd make sure he was fine, and then she'd yell at him for not returning her texts.

Ethan looked at his watch and was pissed to notice his hand was shaking slightly. He adjusted his tie and shifted in his seat as he waited for his doctor to arrive. He was running late. Well, he'd been here for over two freaking hours. The first half hour was his fault, because he'd arrived early. But the last hour and a half was pure torture. This was maybe the most torturous year yet and he knew why—a certain brunette that had a hold on his heart.

Nicholas's untimely arrival Saturday night had been a blessing of sorts, as much as he hated to admit it. He never should've kissed Allie, because he'd end up breaking her heart. Nicholas's appearance reminded him of exactly why he couldn't be involved with Allie. It would be underhanded of him. There was no way to reconcile his want to beat his brother and his feelings for Allie. He'd been dismissed long ago, but he was strong and the team of people he had working on this development would prove to be far superior to Carson's.

Now all he had to do was get a clean bill of health, which was reason number two he was glad things hadn't gotten any farther with Allie. All his defenses had been down that night. Yes, he'd wanted her, that wasn't the part that surprised him. It was the emotional level that floored him. Their conversation, her opening up to him, had rattled him. But he'd abandoned her after in favor of a meeting with his lawyer.

Since moving in, he'd repeatedly failed her. First was Haven House. If she even knew how involved he was in that mess, she would probably kill him with her bare hands—or get her sister to do it. Second was acting like some sort of asswipe when he caught her in his office. And third was ditching her the night she'd made some roundabout plans with him, and he'd been too stupid to even realize it. But he didn't want to share any of that with her. He didn't even like remembering. He never even spoke of it, not to his family, not to his friends, and certainly not to Allie.

Then again, if there were ever a person he could imagine telling, it would be her. He knew why she was so good at her job, why the kids gravitated to her. She had the wisdom of someone much older and the compassion of a saint. But the last thing he would want was her pity.

He tensed as the sound of footsteps approached. Seconds later he was staring at the doctor he only saw once a year and looking for any signs of bad news. Before he could dwell, his doctor was smiling and sitting down with a sigh.

"Sorry to keep you waiting, Ethan. I know you get worried

about these tests. I'm happy to say everything looks good as usual. You couldn't be in any better health."

The massive weight of the chains it felt like he'd been carrying the last month slowly eased, his body feeling lighter. He looked into his doctor's familiar blue eyes, seeing the truth in them. "So, I guess this is it till next year?"

Dr. Peterson slowly stood. "You have yourself a Merry Christmas, Ethan."

Ethan smiled, shook his hand, and left the room. This feeling, it happened to him every year, thankfully. He always came here alone despite his entire family knowing that this was what he did every year. No one had ever offered to come with him, and that was for the best. He didn't like talking or sharing or feelings. Luckily neither did his parents or brother.

He pressed the down button on the elevator repeatedly. While he waited for the elevator to arrive he pulled out his phone and noticed the missed messages from Allie, each getting more frantic with the last one in all caps, demanding he answer her. He stepped into the elevator, smiling.

He frowned as he made his way to the lobby doors and noticed the familiar, gorgeous profile of a brunette standing outside, shoving a cinnamon bun in her mouth. She turned around and made eye contact with him the second he stepped foot on the sidewalk. She stood there, icing on the sides of her lips, her nose red, cheeks pink, and eyes that were filled with…tears.

"Allie, what are you doing here?" He didn't want her to know, he didn't want to share that weakness; he didn't like feeling exposed.

She glared at him through her tears and waved her hand in front of her face, pointing to her mouth. It was currently on the verge of exploding. A second later she opened her mouth. "I remembered on your calendar that today was D-Day, and that's a very ominous thing to write down, you know. I kept calling you at the office, but Ann refused to give me any info until finally Hannah gave me some pointers on finding out details. So I came here, not that I know where here is, but I've been freezing my ass off trying to be supportive and—"

He kissed her, in the middle of the sidewalk, with the crowds bustling by. He kissed her because she was beautiful, she was real, and she actually, genuinely gave a shit about him. He kissed her and tasted the cinnamon, the sugar, and the woman. This would be his undoing—her following him here. He wanted to bury himself in her, absorb the sweetness she embodied. He wanted to feel her legs wrap around him and never let go; he wanted her to keep him here, forever, in this life with her. He wanted to let himself be the kind of man who needed another person. Allie was his greatest fantasy, his greatest weakness.

"Come home with me," he whispered against her lips.

"I live with you."

"Where's your sister?"

"Sandra is no longer dead. They are BFFs again, so she's over at her house."

"Let's go."

"I feel like celebrating," Ethan said as soon as they walked into his condo.

Allie watched as he popped open a bottle of champagne.

"So everything went…well?"

"Better than well. Awesome." He handed her a glass of champagne.

"I'd love to say a toast, but I have no idea what we're toasting because apparently you think I'm this moron who follows you around the city and does not deserve to be let into whatever…challenges you are facing."

He took a long drink. She waited.

"Of course I don't think you're a moron. You're the most perfect woman I've ever met," he said, taking a step into her. She backed up and held up her hand.

"Hold it right there. No attempts at charming me. I want the truth. All of it."

The muscles in his jaw clenched a few times while his gaze locked onto hers, and she wondered if he was evaluating her or if he'd made up his mind already. "I know I can trust you," he said gruffly. "There are things I can't talk about to anyone."

"Am I just anyone?"

She held her breath and realized his answer meant the world to her. "You are so much more to me than you could possibly know, Allie." Ethan's voice was low, raw, and she felt a warmth spread through her.

"What's D-Day?"

He ran his hands through his already scruffy hair and swore softly, walking over to the windows. The moonlight and city lights illuminated his body as he stood there. He looked like an imposing figure, all hard lines and muscle.

Ethan's back was to her. Even the sight of the plump, fluffy snowflakes falling outside the window didn't distract her. She couldn't look beyond him or think of anything other than him and what he was about to tell her—if he actually told her. She sat down on the couch and drew her knees up to her chest and wrapped her arms around them, wanting to feel warm again.

Ethan cleared his throat and finished off his champagne before setting his glass down on the side table. She didn't think he'd turn to look at her, but he did. His hands were stuffed in his pockets. He looked completely beautiful and completely unapproachable. All the hard lines she'd admired were now taut with the tension of whatever it was he was holding in.

"When I was eight I was diagnosed with leukemia."

A wave of goose bumps and nausea rushed over her. She had known on maybe some level, but she hadn't wanted to be right. She wanted to go back to the way they were in bed. She wanted to see his face filled with intense passion or laughing. She didn't want to hear this other voice. It was filled with a hardness she didn't associate with Ethan.

Tears filled her eyes immediately, but she forced herself to hold it all in. She wrapped her arms tightly around herself, trying not to shake. For a second she wondered if she should approach him, but he looked too solitary, too standoffish to approach. He was looking straight into her eyes now, and she wouldn't let him see her cry, so she blinked until she pulled herself together. Acid swirled around in her stomach. She searched for the right words, but shock kept her lips tightly closed. The books she'd seen in his office. It all made sense. Finally, she spoke the only words that came to her. "I'm sorry."

He gave an almost imperceptible shrug, but his brown eyes were locked onto hers and he stared, assessing. She had the uncomfortable feeling that he was assessing her reaction.

"But you're okay now, right?" she whispered after another tense moment.

He walked over to the liquor cabinet and held up a bottle of scotch in her direction. She shook her head. "Still have nightmares from my spiked eggnog."

He almost smiled, but he turned from her and the sound of the liquid being poured into the crystal glass seemed to thunder in the quiet space. She had no idea if he was going to answer her question or just change the subject or walk out of the room. He took a long drink and then placed the empty glass on the end table. "Yeah. I'm fine."

"What's D-Day?" She knew she was pushing, but he wasn't offering. She felt as though she was so close to knowing this other Ethan, and if she didn't uncover all of him now she never would.

He shoved his hands in his pockets and stood in front of the windows. He was all towering strength, at one with the backdrop of the city skyscrapers.

"I go to a private clinic once a year to get complete blood work and scans done."

"Has there ever been…I mean, you were eight? What happened between then and now?"

He lifted one hand to run through his hair. "I had to do chemo. I had to stay at the hospital. The usual crap."

Tears pricked at the back of her eyes. He'd barely told her a thing, yet he was telling her everything in his voice, in the hard lines of his stiff body. "But I got through it. Had to take medication for a couple years to make sure it didn't come back, had to see doctors for a long time. I don't think anyone in my family actually thought I was going to make it."

"Ethan—"

"Everyone had written me off. The day I was diagnosed was the one that made me different from Carson, the day my father thought I wouldn't be worth the time investment because who knew if I'd be around."

"That can't be true."

"There are things about my family that took me a while to understand. Appearances are everything. But my mother and father have been living separate lives for years, and the whole family bond thing doesn't really exist. My brother and I aren't close. After being sick, it created a bigger divide." He shrugged, rubbing the back of his neck. "We're not like you and Dani. We see each other at family functions. He kisses my dad's ass primarily so he can take over the family business." He stopped talking abruptly.

The vulnerability in his voice tugged at her until the tears came back. She remembered the picture in his office. "What about the little girl in the picture with you?"

He rubbed his hand over his jaw and squeezed his eyes

shut. "Cara. She had a brain tumor. We, uh, became really good friends. I corrupted her," he said with a laugh. "Within days of becoming friends, I taught her how to sneak extra desserts from the kitchen, and taught her how to ride a skateboard down the hospital hallway."

She was trying to smile even though tears were rolling down her face. She swiped them as Ethan paused and took another drink. "You do have a way with the ladies," she attempted to joke.

He gave her a little half-smile. "She was in there a lot longer than I was. She had a special…" His voice trailed off, and he looked down. "Sort of like what you have. That warmth, that special glow. I guess I realized at an early age how to spot a winner," he said with a short laugh. "I asked her to marry me while we were eating contraband Jell-O in the kids' lounge."

Her voice was trapped and she stared at him, already knowing what he was going to say next even though she didn't want to hear it.

"What did she say?"

One corner of his mouth curled up. "She agreed, but only after I begged for like a week. I also had to bribe her with Jell-O every day."

She laughed softly, picturing the two of them.

His smile fell, and he downed the contents of his glass. "But, uh, Cara didn't make it."

"I'm so sorry, Ethan."

He gave a nod, looking down.

"The bracelet?"

He nodded. "She gave it to me when I left the hospital."

She was not going to cry again. She wasn't, even though she thought it was the sweetest thing in the world. Thinking of Ethan as this little boy going through cancer with indifferent and cold parents broke her heart. The whole image he portrayed to the world was not the man he really was. He had a sensitivity and compassion that made her heart ache.

"And the prayer?"

He ran his hands down his face with a sigh. "From Nurse Annie. Apparently I was a bit of a control freak, even at that point in my life. I would interrogate the doctors and nurses, and I was always really worried about Cara. I basically drove myself crazy and the medical staff as well."

"I can imagine," she said, forcing a small smile.

"One night, Annie came into my room and handed me that slip of paper. She asked me to read it aloud."

"And?"

"I didn't get it. I told her I didn't believe in God. My parents didn't believe in God. So I just thought her prayer was a nice gesture, and I thanked her."

"What did she say?"

He gave the faintest hint of a smile. "She sat down on my bed and said that it was okay I didn't believe in God, and that my family didn't, and she didn't want to make me feel bad. In my infinite wisdom at the age of eight, I told her no offense was taken, and I didn't think any less of her for believing in fairy tales and omniscient beings. And then I told her I wouldn't let her secret out, because people might think less of her. It was a hospital filled with doctors and nurses and everyone believed in science and facts, so how could she possibly believe in something that had no scientific evidence? I was worried they'd hold it against her."

Allie shook her head, smiling.

"I know, right?" he said to her with a small smirk. "Talk about ego."

"So what did she say?"

He paused for a long time, staring up at the ceiling, his Adam's apple bobbing a few times before he spoke. "She said, first off, she wasn't ashamed in what she believed in, and that we should be proud of what we believe, even if others don't agree. And then she said it didn't matter if I believed in God or went to church, but that there are some points in a person's life when the need to believe in something bigger, something greater, takes over. She said sometimes the burden of carrying it all alone just gets too great. She said it was okay, she was here for me now, but that when I was on my own again, if I ever needed comfort or if I ever lost my way or the burden was too great, all I needed to do was read these words and feel them, believe them."

Allie wiped the tears that fell onto her face. When his eyes locked onto hers, her heart squeezed when she saw the tears there.

"I never thought I'd believe those words. I never imagined being weak enough to need a prayer or a belief in something greater."

She didn't say anything, sensing he wasn't finished.

"When I found myself thinking about Cara, I read it. I was scared shitless of dying after I went back home, and I didn't know who to talk to. So I'd go to bed with her bracelet and with the prayer. I take it with me every year when I go for my checkup."

"Do you still see Nurse Annie?"

He shook his head. "I've never been back."

"You've never been back to SickKids?"

"I had to go for follow-ups for a few years, but then after that, no. I just…I don't want to go back. I make donations to them, but I can't bring myself to revisit that time in my life when I was so vulnerable. I never want to feel that again, Allie."

She wanted to walk over to him and kiss him.

She wanted to hold on to the man he'd become, the little boy he once was.

She wanted to kiss him with every ounce of love she felt

for him.

She didn't want him to think she pitied him, but she wanted to walk up to him and wrap him up in her arms. She wanted to reach out and comfort the little boy who must have been so scared, who lost the little girl he cared so much for. She wanted to tell him it would be okay, that he would find someone else to love, and he would live a long, happy life. But she couldn't do that. How could she tell him that he would find someone else to love? She wanted to be the one he loved. But she wouldn't say that. Instead, she stood. She walked across the room, and it suddenly felt like he was miles away and each step she took held some significance other than the obvious. Ethan stood still, as though assessing her motive. His brown eyes were steady on hers, the only movement in the rhythmic clenching of his jaw.

She stopped walking when she was in front of him, close enough that if she leaned forward her mouth would reach him. All she knew was that she wanted to be close to him. She tilted her head up to look at him. Then she put her hand on his heart, feeling its strong beat, seeing the vulnerability on his beautiful face as he stood perfectly still and watched her.

"I don't want your pity."

She smiled. "You don't have my pity. You have my admiration, Ethan," she whispered and then kissed the hollow at his throat.

Ethan looked down at the woman in his arms. She was killing him. He'd just had some sort of cathartic experience in which he actually made himself vulnerable to her. She had somehow managed to shred through all his defenses, all the walls he'd built, and strip him down to the essence of who he was. She knew everything—almost everything. If she knew who was really behind the purchase of her precious shelter, she'd walk right out of here without looking back, probably after a swift kick to his ass.

"Allie…" She touched his face with what felt like compassion. He usually hated compassion because it went hand in hand with pity. But her kind of compassion was different. Her eyes were all soft, shiny. Her hands were on him, and she was looking up at him as though she knew the kind of man he really was and wanted him despite it.

He stopped her, covering her hand with his. That was a mistake because she looked up at him, blue eyes filled with determination. Her skin was soft beneath his, and the feel of her so close to him was making him forget everything. He'd find a way to fix things later.

She stood on her tiptoes, leaned into him, and kissed his neck. "Ethan," she said against his skin. "I'm sorry for every single time I turned you down. I'm sorry for doubting the kind of man you are. Just don't say no to me. Your ego is more than capable of handling rejection, but mine wouldn't be able to take it."

He was done. He gently fisted his hands in her hair, taking one last look at her. Her lips were parted, lush; her eyes were heated, and he knew there was no going back. "As if I'd ever say no to you," he whispered roughly before taking her mouth in his. He kissed her long and wet and deep. He moved his hands from her hair to her shoulders, trailing down, tracing her body. He picked her up, and she straddled him as he carried her into his bedroom, kicking the door shut behind him.

"Lock it," she said between kisses.

"Good idea," he said and backed up to do so, her legs wrapped tightly around him.

He dropped her onto the bed and followed her down. Her fingers trailed over him and he knew there would be no walking away from Allie.

Allie forgot to breathe as Ethan's body covered hers. Her head pressed into the pillow, and he proceeded to kiss her as though he were starving. He kissed her with an intensity that hadn't been there before. Every inch of her body felt as though he lighted it.

"I've wanted you for so long," he whispered against her skin, his stubble grazing her chin. Then his hands were at the hem of her sweater and she lifted her arms up, helping him take it off. "You're beautiful." Just the look in his eyes made her ache for more of him.

"Your turn," she said, and quickly undid the buttons, already knowing what she'd find underneath. She splayed open the shirt, her hands trailing down over his hard chest, her fingertips tracing his abs and stopping at his belt.

"We're not rushing. We haven't waited this long to rush," he said, taking her mouth in a long, wet, deep kiss that left them both breathless. But despite his declaration, his hands were everywhere, then his mouth was everywhere, and then all their clothes were gone.

"You feel so good," she whispered against his mouth. Her hands glided over his wide shoulders then the sculpted muscles of his body to cup his butt. His chest was warm and hard against hers, but then he was moving again. His mouth began a glorious journey and soon she was clutching his head to her as he licked her nipple, his tongue grazing the tip and then sucking until she cried out. She arched against him, feeling his rock hard erection against her, needing more.

"I need all of you, Ethan," she whispered as his finger traced her slowly. She whimpered as his finger slipped inside her.

"God, you're so wet, Allie," he murmured in her ear.

She whimpered, reacting to the raw sound of desire in his voice, to the slow, skilled, movement of his fingers. "It's your fault. This is what happens when we wait so long."

"I would have done this the first night we met."

"And you're always parading around here half-dressed—"

"No, that's when you were spying on me." She stopped speaking because it was too difficult to keep up with the banter when his mouth and fingers were ready to send her over the edge. "Good, we should stop talking now, anyway," he said, because apparently she'd just aired her thoughts aloud. She arched her hips against him and whimpered, before lightly biting his shoulder.

"I'm not doing this alone, Ethan."

"What?" he said against her breast.

"It's not enough. I want you inside me," she whispered against his lips. He let go only long enough to reach for a condom in his nightstand, and then he was back, his mouth on hers, devouring hers, promising exactly what he'd do when he was inside her. She felt as though she'd snap with the tightness she felt, the need that consumed her.

"God, I want you, Allie." She looked up at him, the light from the cityscape falling over him, highlighting just how beautiful he was, how powerful, how perfectly sculpted he was. He slid between her thighs and waited, surely trying to drive her even more insane.

He kissed her long, slow, and deep as he entered her. She gasped and gripped his shoulders at the sensation. He groaned her name as she arched against him, and he angled her hips to his. She met his thrusts, knowing she was on the verge of losing control completely. She wanted more, and he gave it to her. His voice was low, guttural, as he said her name; it was the last sound she remembered as he took her where she needed to be. And then he followed her.

They stayed there, tangled in each other's bodies. After a few seconds, minutes, she didn't really know, Ethan rolled off her, taking her with him.

"Are you sleeping?" she whispered after watching his deep, even breathing for a few minutes. She let her gaze wander over him, again admiring everything about him.

He smiled, his eyes still closed. "I have waited for you, Allie, so long."

She kissed his shoulder and rested her head on his chest. This. Ethan. Everything about him…she loved.

Chapter Eleven

Allie was finishing up some paperwork, excited about leaving. It was almost the end of the day, and this was the weekend they were going up to Jackson and Hannah's cabin. She'd missed her best friend so much and was dying to see the kids, too.

She jumped at the loud knock on her door. Seconds later, Ethan was already inside and shutting the door behind him. He proudly held up a small, live Christmas tree in a black pot.

"What's this?" Allie asked, getting up from her chair, smiling.

"This is me adding Christmas spirit to your office," he said, placing the potted tree in the corner of her small office. A paper bag fell out of his coat pocket and he grabbed it, looking slightly mischievous as he straightened up.

"What's that?"

He grinned. "Cookies from Hannah. But none of this is really why I came here," he said, crossing the room and pulling her into him. This whole being in a relationship thing with Ethan was all-consuming. "I missed you," he said against her lips. "And I know this weekend at Hannah and Jackson's cabin we're hardly going to get a chance to be alone."

"I have an open-door policy," she said against his lips.

He walked around her, jotted something on a Post-It note, and then whipped open the door. He slapped it on the front and then shut and locked it. Then resumed kissing her.

"What did you write on there?"

He leaned down to kiss her. "'My open-door policy is still in effect. Just knock first and I'll open the door.'"

She laughed until she forgot why she was laughing. Ethan had her pressed up against the door, one hand cupping the side of her face, the other under her sweater and cupping her breast. Her phone buzzed.

"Ignore it," he said, kissing her earlobe. "It's Jackson and Hannah asking what time we're going up."

"What time are we going?"

"I don't know why we get roped into going there every year," he said, helping her as she tried to slide his coat off his shoulders. It landed on the ground with a thud.

"I think it's because we're Em's godparents," she said, fiddling with his tie.

He yanked it off in a second. "Talk about taking advantage of our generosity."

She laughed. "You love being her godfather. You spoil her."

"Yeah, well, she's cute. Too bad her parents are so anal about arranging meals around naptimes." He pulled off her sweater, the blast of cold air quickly replaced by Ethan.

"I really don't think we should be doing this here," she whispered.

"The door's locked. Besides, do you have any appointments?"

"No," she said, her knees wobbling as he started a trail of kisses from her ear down her neck. The hard knock on the door reverberated on her bare back and she jumped. Ethan swore.

"What are the freaking odds of this?"

"I knew I shouldn't have listened to you!" she said as he tossed her the sweater.

He stuffed his tie in his pocket and put his coat back on, grumbling.

"Okay, do I look normal?" she asked, standing in front of him. The knocking continued.

Ethan nodded, sitting on the edge of her desk.

She swung open the door to find Max standing there. "Hi Max!" She cringed at the sound of her voice, slightly shrill, way too chipper.

Max's gaze darted from her to over her shoulder. She opened the door wider. "Uh, sorry to bug you guys…"

"Nah, come on in. I'm not supposed to be here anyway," Ethan called out before she could answer. Max looked relieved and walked into the room. He looked comfortable with Ethan, and Allie had a vague recollection of the two of them talking during the Christmas tree lighting. "I'm going to head out. Here, want a cookie?"

Allie thought for sure Max would say no, but he looked up at Ethan and accepted one of the cookies he was holding out. "Thanks. Actually, I kinda wanted to talk to you, too. Well, I wasn't going to ask to talk to you…but was going to ask through Allie."

Ethan sat back down on the edge of the desk, snapping the head off the snowman cookie. He held the bag of cookies toward her. She shook her head. She wasn't taking any of his December cookies. "Go ahead, Max," he said, after Max didn't elaborate.

Max looked nervously from her to Ethan. "I, uh, was wondering if you maybe had something I could do at the office. I know it'd be after Christmas and stuff, and I know it'd only be part-time until summer. But I totally get it if you can't."

"Done. Come in on Monday after school, and I'll hook you up with something. Okay?"

Max didn't say anything for a minute then stood up abruptly. "Really?"

Ethan nodded and procured a business card from one of his pockets. "Just go to that address and ask for me." He extended his hand, and Max shook it with obvious gusto.

"Thanks, man…Ethan, I mean. Or Mr…"

"Ethan's good."

Max nodded again and walked toward the door. He shot Allie a smile that made her heart squeeze. "Thanks, Allie." She smiled at him.

"I'll, uh, close the door and go," he said, giving Ethan a pointed look.

Ethan laughed softly as Max stepped out, shutting the door behind him.

Allie turned to Ethan. "You are so sweet. The best, Ethan," she said, walking up to him. She expected him to gloat playfully, or accept the praise with mischievous arrogance. But instead something flashed through his eyes, and his smile dipped slightly.

He pulled her into his arms and hugged her.

"Wait a second," Ethan whispered in her ear. Instead of walking through the open door, he shut it after Dani walked through. He pulled Allie into his arms even though it was freezing. They had arrived at Jackson and Hannah's cottage. He pinned her against the wall and kissed her thoroughly, as though it had killed him to not have privacy in the car ride up here. She held on to him and kissed him back until the door swung open.

Ethan's muffled curse against her mouth made her laugh. "All I wanted was a few minutes to ourselves before the next twenty-four hour ambush."

"Well, you're too late. Haul your ass inside. Hannah made appetizers and there are only two hours until Christopher's bedtime. Hi, Allie."

Allison's gaze went from Ethan's handsome face to Jackson's. "Hi, Jackson," she said, pulling out of Ethan's embrace. She was laughing as she went inside and Emily and Christopher ran up to her. Visiting her best friend and family during the holidays had quickly become her favorite holiday tradition. Even Dani didn't complain about it.

"I'm so glad you're here," Hannah squealed, throwing her arms around her. Allison hugged her back. How far they had come. Working together at the miserable social services office years ago seemed like a distant dream. Allison did miss her friend, but she wouldn't begrudge her an ounce of happiness. Jackson had turned out to be the best thing that could have ever happened. Once nicknamed Scrooge, he turned out to be a guy with a huge heart, and she knew they were blissfully happy.

"Come inside, you need to catch me up on your gossip," her friend said after Jackson had taken her coat. Once the kids were busy attacking "Uncle Ethan," she followed Hannah into the kitchen. The delicious smell of turkey hit her as she entered the small space.

"Oh my God, this smells so good."

"Thanks, but you need to tell me all about living with Ethan."

Allison eyed the containers of berries and marched over to them. "Can I wash and help?"

"Only if you can talk at the same time," Hannah said as she proceeded to slice some bread.

Allison began dumping the berries into a large colander in the sink. How was she going to explain something she didn't even get? She couldn't mention the cancer because she knew Ethan had never told anyone. She sprayed the berries with water and struggled for words. After a few minutes, Hannah appeared at her side and shut off the water.

She glanced over at her friend, who was staring at her. "I think the berries are clean. Ethan?"

Not so clean, she thought, immediately thinking of the things he'd whispered to her last night. She cleared her throat and tried to get her mind back into neutral territory. "Ethan and I are kind of together in a—"

Hannah mouthed a scream. "I've been hoping for this since the beginning! What changed your mind about him?"

Images of Ethan in the condo, the wrapped gifts, the look on his face when he found out about the fire, the way he was with Dani…the way he was with her. "He's not who I thought he was. He's sweet. And hot. Soooo hot," she said before putting her face in her hands. "I'm so screwed, Hannah, we will never work."

Her friend's laughter died quickly. "Of course you will. I don't think he's the kind of guy to just give up. He's had his eye on you since the wedding, according to Jackson."

She glanced over at her. "We come from really different places. And yeah, I may have underestimated the kind of person he is, but that doesn't mean this will ever go anywhere… close to what you and Jackson are."

Hannah didn't say anything for a moment and Allie knew her friend was trying to come up with a convincing argument, except Jackson walked in at that moment.

"I'm told it's time for me to get the turkey on the table. Mr. Sampson said he'll die if he has to keep smelling the food and not eating."

They both smiled. The elderly couple had become very

close to Jackson, Hannah, and the kids and were like surrogate grandparents. Which was sweet, especially since Hannah and Jackson had no biological family. "Okay, point me here and there and I'll help put things on the table," Allie said.

Ten minutes later they were seated around the enormous table. It was a setting straight out of a home and garden magazine. Gold-rimmed china dishes with tiny reindeer prancing around the edges graced each place setting. Sparkling crystal and silverware and an abundance of homemade food filled the rest of the table. The conversation was loud and boisterous—extra loud because for some reason the Sampsons thought Jackson had a hearing problem. Ethan's hand on her knee was the most surprising, and delicious, part of the meal.

This whole Christmas gig at Jackson and Hannah's was always something he looked forward to, but this year with Allie it was the best. Everything about her was the best. The only thing he hadn't figured out was the shelter. Each day that went by he felt himself grow more and more tense.

"Did Ethan tell you he went skating with Allie at Nathan Phillip's Square?"

Jackson's face split into a giant dumb-ass grin. "Ethan went to a public rink?"

Everyone laughed. He kicked his friend under the table. "It wasn't a big deal."

"Allie, I've been meaning to ask you what's happening with the shelter."

Ethan's stomach dropped. Hell. This should not be a topic of conversation. He wasn't ready to answer questions. He didn't have any acceptable answers. He tried to think up something to say, but there was nothing to say without looking suspicious.

Allison frowned and took a sip of wine. "Ugh. No. The landlord is still determined to sell. The last I heard there are different condo companies waiting to bid on it. Next Thursday is when they're taking all offers."

"I can't believe they're going through with it," Hannah said, filling up her wineglass. "I mean, those kids…just getting secure in a safe environment only to have it ripped out from under them."

"What about you, Ethan? I know Allie said you were going to try and see if you could call in some favors."

He cleared his throat and attempted to lie to his best friend's wife. "Yeah—"

Allie interrupted, patting his hand. "Ethan was great. He worked around the clock trying to help out. He even volunteered, and then the donation—"

"It was nothing," he said, feeling like a bigger and bigger asshole the longer this conversation went on.

"You've been busy. So you figure out how you're going to juggle running your dad's company and ours?"

Ethan shot Jackson what he hoped was a shut up scowl.

"What? Running your father's company?"

Ethan glanced over at Allie. She had put down her fork and was watching him. Assessing. He knew she must find it odd that he wouldn't have told her about something like that.

"Ethan's multi-talented," his friend said. He knew he was trying to help. He knew Jackson was aware of the resentment and competitiveness he felt toward his brother, but he had no idea what was happening now, he had no idea that project was Allie's shelter. "Did you and Hayden ever get together for that proposal on Islington and Lakeshore?"

Dani gasped. "What the hell?"

"Language," Allie whispered to Dani. The sound of her voice…he looked over at her and flinched at the accusation on her face, but she didn't say a word. She was presumably waiting for him to say something. Jackson had no idea what was going on.

"What's wrong? I'm not following," Hannah said.

Allie was watching him, doubt clouding her eyes. "I don't know. Maybe Ethan can tell us? This doesn't make any sense. Just because that's where the shelter is, doesn't mean we're talking about the same project. Right?"

Jackson mumbled a curse under his breath. Ethan fought for the words that would make his explanation sound okay. He glanced around the table and knew there wasn't one person seated there who would understand this. Hell, he barely understood it anymore.

"Ethan?" Allie whispered in a voice that broke his damn heart.

He cleared his throat. "It's not exactly what you're thinking. Yeah, technically I entered into a bid for the property—"

"The property being Haven House," Dani said.

His jaw clenched and he looked her squarely in the eyes, cringing at how pissed she looked at him. "Yes. Haven House."

Hannah gasped; Dani swore under her breath. Allie didn't say a word. He looked at her, but she turned away from him. He felt like his insides had just been twisted. Disgust with himself pummeled through him, and he wondered how the hell he'd ever be able to make Allie understand.

"I didn't want to be a part of this project, but it was a family deal. I've been trying to come up with a workaround. Moving the shelter to another location—"

"And you were going to tell me this when?" Allie still didn't look at him when she asked the question.

"When I had it all figured out."

She stood abruptly, and he caught her chair before it tumbled. She stormed out of the house and Ethan ran his hands through his hair. He had to go after her.

"Holy crap, man. What the hell were you thinking?"

Ethan shook his head and walked out the front door without looking at any of them.

Allie was standing on the porch, her back to him, but he heard the sniffles, and the sounds tugged at everything in him. She slowly turned around, her gaze filled with such hurt and anger that he winced, putting his hands in his pockets. If he didn't, he'd make an attempt to reach out and touch her. He knew at that moment, even though it was far too late for the discovery, that disappointing Allie was so much fucking worse than losing to his brother.

"I have nothing to say to you except I want to believe you couldn't be the one behind this. This makes no sense to me. Tell me something; give me anything that could make this right. I want to believe that you couldn't do this."

"It's true, Allie, but I never set out to close the shelter. Hell, I didn't even know what the building was at first. I was given an opportunity to have a shot at the family business. If I didn't take it, my brother would get it."

"So? So what?"

"I couldn't let that happen. I vowed I'd never let him win again. I'd never let him be stronger than me. He's gotten whatever he wanted since we were kids. He wrote me off and took what should have been equally mine."

"So this is where the rich get richer and you ditch everyone you love—everyone who means something to you, for money?"

Every muscle in his body ached as he listened to her and looked at her. Loved. Yeah. He loved her. He knew it now. He had always known she was special, but now he was in love with her, too, and he was killing her. "It's not about money. It's about winning, showing them that I'm strong and relevant."

She paused for a second. "I feel bad for what you went

through, for how your family reacted, and how they weren't there for you. I get it, but no matter what you do it won't change them. You can change, you can be someone who can change the lives of so many people."

"I knew this was something you wouldn't understand."

"I understand I was right about you from the beginning. You lack feeling. You're able to shut things off in order to get what you want. You haven't really let me in. If you cared about me, you would never even contemplate doing something like this. If you had empathy, you would never shut those kids down like that."

She splayed her arms wide, a gust of frigid air blowing out from her mouth into the dark sky. "I'll go in and tell those kids at the shelter that the first real, safe home they've ever had is now lost to them because some spoiled, rich brothers are squabbling over daddy's company. I'm sure they'll understand. And Max and Denise and everyone else you managed to charm? I'm sure they'll forgive you."

He ran his hands over his jaw. "You know this is more than that."

"Really? I don't know anything right now. How long have you known?"

He looked into her eyes. The least she deserved was the truth, even though it was going to break her down. "Since the day you came to live with me."

The sound that escaped her mouth was heartbreaking. He took a step toward her, and she held up her hands. He stopped where he was and watched as she sank down to her knees. He thought she was going to cry, and that would have killed him. Instead, she leaned down and gathered up a giant snow boulder and turned to him. She was going to chuck it at him, and he just stood there. Except the boulder broke in her arms and she squealed as she became covered in snow. He sighed and tried to help her wipe it off herself.

She swatted his hands away. "I never want to feel your hands on my body again."

"Allie."

"No. And if you were any kind of decent person, you never would have slept with me in the first place. You never would have let me have…feelings. You never should have pretended to be this great guy and said all those things."

"I meant everything."

"You *lied* to me. You put yourself and your own needs ahead of all of ours. I was owed, at the very least, the truth."

He knew he'd lost her. There was no coming back from this. He should have listened to himself right from the beginning and left her alone. He never should have touched her. He shouldn't have kissed her that night on the sidewalk. Never should have tasted her or gotten lost in her, because now he knew what it felt like to love Allie, and he was about to discover what life was like without her.

"This doesn't have to be black and white. I can make it up to you. I can buy those kids—"

"*Nothing*. You can't buy your way out of this. You can't *buy* love. I will not make excuses for you. I will not be with a person who can't put love first. All my life, I have been second, if I'm lucky. I have never been anyone's number one. I have made excuses for the people I loved. I have taken whatever they have been willing to give me. No more. I loved you; I believed in you. Nothing you can buy will ever make up for the fact that you lied, that you willingly fed your need to win and put that ahead of everything. You didn't even come to me and confide in me and try and come up with a way to solve this. You just went after everything you wanted and thought pathetic Allie would take whatever scraps you threw at her."

"Don't say that."

She swiped angrily at the tears that poured out of her eyes. "I'm more loyal than Hook. When I love someone, I love them completely, with everything that I am. I loved you, Ethan. I would have given you all of me." She covered her face with her hands and he moved forward, trying to pull her in his arms. He was freaking dying inside. She loved him. She loved him so much, and he'd fucked up badly. She shoved him away and glared at him.

She held out her hand. "Give me your keys."

"What?"

"Give me your keys and at least let me leave. I can't stay here and pretend."

"No, you guys stay. I'll leave."

She stopped for a moment and squeezed her eyes shut. "For the record, I regret everything. I regret ever trusting you. I take back everything I said about you coming through for me. If you cared about me as much as you say you did, you'd never just end things right now. If you were the guy I thought you were, you'd get your shit together and realize that what you're doing is wrong. You'd risk anything for me."

"Allie—"

"Save it," she whispered and walked back inside.

Ethan stood in the snow feeling a heaviness, an ache inside him that he had never felt before. The door slammed shut and then reopened a minute later. Dani.

"Hey! Ethan!"

God. She came running up to him, all hundred pounds of attitude and derision.

"What the hell was that? You're such a hypocrite! You sat there giving me lectures on how to treat my sister. No amount of attitude I gave her comes close to this. You totally betrayed her. You're such a jerk! She trusted you."

"I'm sorry. I'm going to fix this."

"You *can't* fix this. Screw you for pretending to be one of the good guys," she said. Her voice broke and tears ran down her face. She wiped them away angrily and then slammed her heel into his toe before walking away.

He was almost at his car when another voice called out his name. He stood there and waited as his best friend rounded the front of his car. Since Jackson's front yard was lit up like Vegas, he was able to see the surprise in his face. "What the hell, Ethan?"

Ethan shrugged. "What do you want me to say? I had no choice."

"That's stupid. Everyone has choices. You took the asshole choice and decided to backstab the only good woman in your life."

He held on to his friend's angry stare for another minute and then looked away. Since when had Jackson become the reasonable, sensible one in their relationship? "I needed to stick it to Carson. I needed to screw him over and prove that I'm better and smarter than him."

"Are you fucking five years old?"

"You wouldn't understand, so shut up."

"I get that somewhere in that messed up head of yours you thought you could go ahead and have this relationship with Allie, who is so in love with you, even I can see it, and then go behind her back and be the person closing down the shelter she's poured her heart into."

"It didn't have to go down like this. I have something else for those kids lined up and you know what, Jackson? Who the hell are you to judge anyway? I remember when Hannah first came into your life with Emily."

"Nope. Not even close to being the same thing because I realized I was wrong—way, way earlier than you. Hell, I don't even know if you get it now."

Ethan resisted the urge to punch his best friend in the face. He couldn't. It wouldn't be fair to Hannah and the kids if their dad went back inside with a black eye. "I need to get out of here. Tell Hannah I'm sorry about dinner."

Chapter Twelve

Ethan paused a moment as he stepped out of the elevator and into the hallway. Perspiration trickled down his back, and his palms felt sweaty. These symptoms were usually saved for his once a year at the clinic, but the last few days he'd been feeling all kinds of crazy things because of Allie, or because he didn't have her anymore.

Before her he thought he'd had everything figured out. He knew what he wanted out of life and he was happy with the person he'd become, the accomplishments he'd achieved. But now, since her, he'd come to realize he didn't know shit, really. The guy she wanted him to be, he wanted to be as well, but he had a few things to get done first before he could prove it to himself and to her.

He took a deep breath, rolled his shoulders, and walked into the hospital wing that was named after him. He pulled the trolley behind him as he walked forward to face his past. The hustle and bustle was the same as he remembered, but that was about it. The place had changed since he was a kid. He wrote a check once a year—the first year a massive one, which had resulted in the wing being in his name. Because writing a check was easier than actually visiting, putting himself out there.

He didn't know what he was doing here, but he did know that it had something to do with finally coming to peace with his past, with the kid he'd been, and finally moving forward. It was time for him to let go of this, and this was the catalyst for the distance and problems he'd had with his brother and family since.

The smell of cleaning products filled his nose as his eyes landed on a group of kids sitting in a circle, listening to a woman read a book to them. There was a big Christmas tree, and the kids were sitting on a rug. The woman looked like a volunteer. His gut clenched and waves of heat rushed through him as he focused on the kids, a couple with those damn scarves wrapped around their heads. He wanted to run out of here, on the treadmill. But he'd been running his whole life, away from emotion.

He didn't know what made him come here today. Maybe it was losing Allie, or maybe it was because he didn't give a rat's ass about the condo deal anymore. He didn't know… anything, except that he missed Allie more than anything or anyone in his entire life. And he knew that if he stood a chance in hell at getting her back, he was going to have to figure out the shit in his past. So, that was what he was doing here. He was going to deal with the kid he was. He didn't like facing it: the memories, the fear.

He walked over to the story center, listening to the volunteer's soft voice as she read *The Night Before Christmas*. Her voice was melodic, following the rhythm perfectly, her smile comforting as she'd look out at the kids. He swallowed past the lump in his throat, remembering how it felt to be here at Christmas, sitting on that rug. Or lying in his hospital room, wondering if Santa would find him there. He remembered the letter he'd mailed him, giving him his new, temporary address. A little blonde girl giggled and the sound ran through him, picking up traces of Cara's laughter, kicking up memories of her.

He'd convinced Cara to write a letter to Santa as well. Christmas morning, he'd woken to his nanny placing a bunch of gifts by his bed and knew he was doomed. If there was no Santa, his wish wouldn't be coming true. His parents didn't believe in any higher power; he hadn't ever prayed a second in his life. All he knew at that moment was that he was on his own. He ran down the hall to Cara's room and found her still sleeping, only one gift beside her bed. So he grabbed a stuffed bear from his pile and a Nerf gun, and placed it with hers. He sat beside her while she slept, thinking he wouldn't tell her Santa was a fake, thinking one day he'd get married to her when they were both better and all grown up. In the meantime, he'd teach her how to use the Nerf gun. That was the last Christmas he saw her.

A hand on his arm knocked him back into the present, and he looked down at the elderly nurse. It took him a moment, a long moment, but the shiver that raced up his spine, the goose bumps that ran rampant over him, told him who she was. Her faded blue eyes still twinkled and held more warmth in them than a hot chocolate.

"I was hoping I'd get a chance to see you today. I knew you were coming," she whispered, her hand still on his arm.

He couldn't speak, because in his throat were all the words he couldn't voice, didn't know how to express. Instead, he leaned down and hugged the woman who'd shown him more kindness than his own parents. He had to squeeze his eyes shut for a moment as he held her in his arms. "Nurse Annie," he finally managed.

She pulled back, beaming, holding on to his arms. "Look at you, all grown up. I knew you'd be back to see me. And I knew you'd be a heartbreaker."

He forced a smile on his face. Yeah. Heartbreaker was right. He broke the heart of a woman as sweet as Allie, and for that he would have to repent. "I've got some presents I thought I'd deliver."

She looked at the dolly behind him and nodded. "I'll help you put them under the tree, but when we're done, you're buying me a coffee in the cafeteria, and then you're going to tell me how life has been to you."

Half an hour later he was sitting across from Annie in the cafeteria. They had found a window seat and she'd finished showing him pictures of her grandchildren.

"Lucky kids," he said, smiling.

She took a sip of her coffee. "Why don't you tell me about you, Ethan? No wedding band I see. I would've thought you'd be married with a truckload of kids."

He shook his head and put his coffee down. "Haven't really made that a priority."

"Hmm…as I recall you didn't have a problem proposing to women or not taking no for an answer."

Yeah, except he'd pissed off the only woman he'd ever propose to. "Well, I did find someone, but uh, I'm not really sure I can make it work."

She leaned forward and gave him the same look she did when she suspected someone had been stealing Jell-O. "Can't or won't?"

He averted his gaze and focused on the Christmas tree in front of the window. "She has…ideals…"

"Usually that's a trait people admire," she said with a deep frown.

"I know. She reminds me of you."

She wagged a finger at him. "Don't go trying to charm me with your flattery. Tell me what you did so I can guide you back to her, Ethan."

He laughed and groaned at the same time. He told her the details surrounding his father's competition, and she sat there, silent for a long time.

"Did you tell your father what this would mean for you? For Allie?"

He knew she wouldn't understand. "That's irrelevant to him, Annie. Business and personal don't mix."

"So then, how are you feeling? Do you feel as though you made the right choice? You lied to a woman you love deeply, you made friends with the kids at the shelter, and then you backstabbed all of them by putting your own personal needs first. How is that working for you, Ethan?"

He ran his hands down his face. "Shit, Annie, you're still a ball-breaker."

She chucked a cookie at him. "You should have been back here to visit me sooner. I would have set you straight before you screwed everything up."

He took a bite of the cookie she threw at him, not even enjoying it. He didn't enjoy anything without Allie. He missed her in his house; he missed her in his bed. He missed visiting her at the shelter. Hell, he was miserable.

"Come follow me, and then I need to get back to my shift."

They walked out the lobby and through the front doors. It was snowing, the day dark and damp. Annie was made of steel, barely a shiver as she walked to a quiet spot near a tall spruce. "Nothing like a snowy day, the anticipation of Christmas in the air," she said, breathing deeply and looking up at the sky. Ethan didn't want to tell her this was actually crap weather despite the time of year. He shoved his hands in his pockets.

"Do you remember the prayer?" Annie asked after a few minutes of watching cars drive by.

His stomach dropped. He nodded.

She turned to him, jaw set. "Then say it."

"Say what?"

"The words."

"Now?"

She nodded. He sighed roughly.

"Annie…"

"Ethan."

"God grant me the serenity to accept the things I cannot change, courage to change the things I can, and the wisdom to know the difference."

She didn't say anything for a long moment, a sheen entering her eyes. He attempted to clear his throat; he knew the both of them were thinking of that night, of Cara. Annie had read it to him that night. He had never read the words out loud.

She took hold of his hand. He squeezed it gently, noting how much frailer it felt than when he'd been a kid. "Make it up to her, Ethan. Don't lose her."

Sunday brunch at his parents, the week before Christmas; this one would go down in the record books. Maybe a part of him never really wanted to know. Maybe a part of him was comfortable in not knowing or not feeling.

He took a sip of orange juice and stared across the table at his mother, father, and brother.

"Ready for tomorrow's presentation, Ethan?"

He smiled at Carson, ready to get this done and over with. Ready to rip off the Band-Aid. "Actually, I wanted to talk to you about that, Dad."

His father looked up from his plate of smoked salmon and fruit salad.

"I know you're putting in your offer tomorrow, and I'd like to ask you to change the usage of the building."

His father frowned. "Get to the point."

"I want you to keep it as a shelter."

Carson choked on his orange juice.

"That's absurd. Why would I do that?"

"There's a shelter—"

"I'm not about to outbid all the other developers only to house a shelter. That's suicide and makes no business sense whatsoever. I would never pay that kind of money for a shelter."

Ethan knew this was a long shot. He knew it didn't make business sense, he knew the kind of money it was going to take to be the highest bid. "Then I'm asking you as a personal favor."

Everyone stopped eating. His mother looked concerned. His father looked pissed. Carson looked smug.

"You didn't get the proposal done, did you?" Carson asked, leaning back in his chair, tilting it on only two legs. Ethan resisted the urge to shove it over, as he'd done on numerous occasions in his youth.

"Why on earth would you ask me that?"

Ethan turned to his father and tried to put this whole feelings thing to use in a family that had none. "I'm in love with a woman who works at the shelter."

"This is priceless. You're in love with a homeless person!" Carson tipped his chair back farther, hands in the air. Ethan nudged the one leg, pushing it over and watched with satisfaction as his brother tipped backward.

"Boys, please stop," his mother said as Carson swore and righted himself.

"First off, she's not homeless, she *works* there. Secondly, the kids in that place are trying to get their lives straightened out. They lack security and to force them out is cruel."

"So this worker put you up to this?"

Ethan stared at his father's dispassionate face, not an

ounce of emotion in his eyes and thought of Allie and her abundance of emotion. The night at Jackson and Hannah's when she threw snow at him, when she basically looked at him as though she had no idea who he was, certainly not with any of the warmth from before. "She didn't put me up to anything. I'm here because I realized the only reason I went along with this is because I wanted to be part of the family business, but not enough to ignore what's right."

His mother put down her napkin, her face pulled into a frown as far as the Botox would allow. "My dear, there was always a place for you."

"No, there wasn't. I was basically ignored after what happened…when I had cancer."

His father didn't say anything, his jaw just clenched. At least the man wasn't a liar.

"Regardless of what you think, I can't do what you're asking of me."

Ethan stared into his father's face, his features remarkably similar to his own. "I'll ask you one last time, for me, as your son, please don't go through with the development project."

His father broke his stare, cut a piece of smoked salmon, looped a red onion around his fork, and looked up at him. "No, and never ask me something so pathetic again. Weakness like that will get you killed in business." Ethan studied his father, looking for an ounce of softening. He hadn't changed. If having a child with cancer didn't change you, then nothing could. It's not that he sought comfort from him, or that he expected him to become all schmaltzy, but maybe a moment of entertaining the idea or really listening to him.

If they could so easily dismiss his request, then he'd be forced to do the same.

Ethan sat in his car outside his parent's house and dialed Nicholas Wright's phone number. Having friends in all the right places came in handy. You could call on Sundays and not be billed. "Nick, I need the name of the best commercial real estate agent you know."

"Why?"

"I'm not going through with the proposal. I'm going to put in my own bid."

"Against your dad's company?"

"Yeah. I'd love to chat, but I need to move on this tomorrow. I need an agent who can put this deal together for me now."

Nicholas sighed. "There's only one agent that comes to mind. She's the best of the best. Hot but really irritating, and I'm forced to work with her way more—"

"I don't have time to hear your analysis of this woman. Text me her details," he said and ended the call. As soon as the text came through, he took the next step in making all of this right, in getting Allie back.

Chapter Thirteen

"I'm not telling them. I refuse. Even though I know it's inevitable, I think we should wait until after the holidays. They need to have a good Christmas," Allie said, clearing more dishes from the empty tables. The fact that she was even coherent was a miracle.

Every single moment since Ethan had basically ripped her heart out of her chest and stomped on it, she'd been torn between crying and yelling at herself for being so stupid. Even her sister was being nice to her because she felt so sorry for her. After their night at Hannah and Jackson's she went back to the condo, grabbed their things, and found a decent hotel with a weekly rate. She had found them a new apartment, and they were ready to move in next week. Just in time for Christmas. Yay.

"You're right. We'll keep this quiet until after the holidays are over. Are we all set with the presents?"

Allie nodded. "Yup." Allie watched her sister laugh in the gathering room with some of the other kids. She was happy Dani was here tonight, keeping her company. Again, another sign her sister pitied her.

The bell at the front desk rang, and she followed Denise out. Even when it was late at night they accepted new teens. Sometimes it was the most popular time, especially in the winter. The thought of another night on the street with frigid temperatures was the final thing that brought them in. But it wasn't a teen.

It was Ethan.

She was completely immune to the man, she told herself. He was standing there with boxes and boxes filled with wrapped gifts. She crossed her arms. Denise inhaled sharply and then walked forward and poked him in the chest. "Are these the gifts you plan on handing out before you take everyone's house away from them?"

He smiled. He was wearing jeans and a hoodie, and he had stubble. And the ratty Blue Jays cap. His eyes sparkled and, oh God, she was such a liar for telling herself she was immune to him. Even though it was "Weekend Ethan" and he was her favorite Ethan, she refused to acknowledge the way her heart beat like an out of control drum.

"No. They are staying. The shelter is staying."

Denise gasped.

Allie stared at him, wanting so much to believe him but needing more. "How is that possible?"

"I put in a bid, on my own. I outbid my brother."

Tears blurred her vision for a moment. She blinked them away. "What does that mean?"

"It means it took me a little longer than it should have to come up with a solution, but it was the only solution, because not having you in my life wasn't an option for me. And being a guy obsessed with revenge isn't an option for me. Having you disappointed in me killed me. Not waking up to you, not going to bed with you…not an option."

"You seem pretty confident there for a guy who royally

screwed up."

He grinned and walked toward her. "I will spend the rest of the night and the rest of my life making it up to you. I know I disappointed you, and I let you down."

She was a blubbering mess now, and it was impossible to go from pretending she hated the man to professing her undying love to him. "You killed me. You made me believe that all my instincts had been wrong. You made me trust you, you made me think you had my back and then you just betrayed me, Ethan." She was vaguely aware of Denise shutting the dining room door behind her and leaving. She covered her face with her hands, and Ethan whispered her name in a delicious, gravelly voice. He pulled her into his arms and kissed the top of her head. "I love you, Allie, and I've got your back forever."

"Did you really buy this place?" she mumbled against him.

She felt him nod.

"You got hosed with the price, didn't you?"

"Completely. Worst financial investment I've ever made in my entire life. Best personal one though, by a long shot."

She wrapped her arms around him tightly and looked up. His hands softly framed her face. "It's going to take a lot more than overpaying for me to win back your trust, isn't it?"

She studied him, the truth in his eyes, the love. She shook her head and smiled. "I think you've proven yourself."

He leaned down and kissed her, and it felt like she'd been without him for years, when it had only been days. Ethan had somehow found his way inside her soul and heart. He was the rock she had always wanted, the person who would come through for her in the end. She knew what it had meant for him to let go of his grudge, to finally allow himself to be the person he was meant to be. He kissed her until she was weak in the knees and forgot that she was in Haven House. "I love you," he whispered again.

"I love you, too," she said, finally saying the words that felt so right.

"Oh my God, Allie are you *insane*?"

Allie groaned and set her forehead on Ethan's shoulder. Her sister.

Ethan slowly turned around to face Dani. Max was standing beside her, scowling. "Dani, before you go attacking me, you should know I fixed everything. This place isn't closing."

Dani didn't say anything for a moment, and Allie waited for some smart-ass comment, but it didn't come. Max was looking at her, clearly not knowing what to do. Finally Dani spoke. "Well, good. I'm glad you figured it out…" Her voice trailed off for a second, and Allie caught the faint quiver in her sister's chin. "I'm…you came through for Allie, and she needed that. *You*. She needs you."

Ethan broke out into a grin, and Allie was shocked when her sister ran up and gave him a hug. "And good move coming in here with gifts."

Ethan laughed, pulling back. "Yeah, I figured the gifts might go over well."

"I want you to know I'm really happy Ethan didn't turn out to be a total douchebag," Dani said.

Allie nodded, "Thanks. Me too."

"And it's cool that he did all this, like the gifts and stuff. I think he wrapped them himself because I see bunched up tape all over the sides."

Allie laughed. "Yeah, but he gets an A for effort."

"You know I'm still standing here, right?" Ethan asked.

"I, uh, think I'll go open presents," Max said awkwardly. "Allie?"

Her heart squeezed at the sound of Max using her name for the first time. She reigned in her feelings and nodded.

"I'm glad things worked out for you guys."

"Thanks, Max."

He shrugged and left the room.

"I'll be back in a second," Ethan said, kissing her. "I want to make sure those gifts get distributed properly."

"Ethan's really cool," Dani said, after Ethan left the room. She was arranging her long hair over one shoulder and then running her fingers through it. Allie eyed her sister. Something was up.

"I'm glad you approve."

Her sister gave her a distracted smile, and Allie could see she was hiding something.

"And I'm really happy you guys are together again."

"And?"

Dani let out a sigh. It wasn't her usual theatrical sigh. This one seemed genuine, and her lips were downturned.

"Hey, Dani. Tell me, what's up?"

"Nothing." She looked down at her feet. "I don't want to have to go back to mom's, you know? But I will, I mean, like, if Ethan doesn't want me around."

Allie felt tears at the back of her eyes. Dani never showed vulnerability. "You're my sister, and if you think I'd just ditch you—"

"You're family, Dani." Ethan was standing in the doorway, his brown eyes filled with tenderness as he looked at her younger sister. "You stay with us, even if I have to get another job to support your shopping habits."

Her sister smiled slightly and looked over at him. "I don't want to be the loser mooch that you're forced to support. Though if you are having financial difficulties, it's probably due to the fact that you totally overpaid for this place."

He laughed. "I think I'll manage, and we can't exactly kick you to the curb. You've gotten used to a certain lifestyle, and I've gotten used to having you around."

Her sister crossed her arms and jutted her chin out. "Yeah, I guess I keep you guys young."

Ethan grinned. "If I had a little sister I think I'd want her to be a ball-breaker like you."

Her sister broke out into a grin. "My sister has turned you into a sap."

He shrugged. "Maybe, but that's okay. I think I'm ready."

E than waited for Allie to get her coat. They were going home, and he couldn't wait to have her alone. He hadn't slept in days, but he felt alive, and so damn good. Maybe that's what happened when you made the right decisions and people you actually loved surrounded you. Feelings weren't overrated. Huh.

"Yo, Ethan?"

Ethan turned around to look at Max. The kid looked better, less like a delinquent and more like a typical teenager. "I wanted to say thanks for the iPad. That was pretty cool of you."

Ethan shrugged. "You're welcome. Glad you like it."

"Allie had said we all get Christmas presents here. That was cool. I didn't know what to expect when I came here, you know? Like, there's lots of rules and shit, but it's better than where I came from."

A lump formed in Ethan's throat. My God, he *was* becoming a giant sap, maybe even as big as Jackson now. "Don't forget to come by my office if you still want that job."

Max nodded, the expression on his face making his gut clench. The kid looked so damn surprised, almost overwhelmed. "Thanks. I uh, will."

"But you can't hit on Allie."

Max grinned at him. "It's okay. I was thinking her sister is more my type anyway."

Dani presented herself in the doorway, all attitude and sly smiles. "Hey, douchebag, you're supposed to help me clear the table."

Max shrugged and followed Dani out of the room, a small smile tugging at the corner of his mouth. Allie hurried down the hallway toward him in her coat and hat. She grabbed his hand and dragged him out the front door. They stopped in front of his car. The street was quiet and snow was tumbling from the sky.

"We've got exactly three hours before Dani gets home."

He grinned and stepped into her, dipping his head so that he could taste her again. She tasted different tonight, she tasted like she was his, like she would be his, forever. "Ah, so you're dying to get me back to the condo so you can—"

"It's the whole Weekend Ethan thing you've got going on. And maybe the fact that you blew a fortune saving a shelter."

"A minor detail." He laughed as he kissed her. He sank his fingers into her thick hair and kissed her like he'd never get enough of her, but he already knew that. He knew he'd never get enough of Allie. Allie had brought him back to the person he was meant to be, the guy he'd buried years ago. She took away his fear. She made him whole. She made him real.

"Merry Christmas, Allie," he whispered against her lips.

Epilogue

"What's the point of being rich if you can't get a giant church in the city to get married in? I mean, seriously, we're out in the sticks."

Allie laughed at her sister's disgruntled expression. "This was a sentimental choice, Dani."

"Oh, right," Dani mumbled, giving Hannah a small, slightly sheepish smile.

The three of them, along with Emily and Christopher, were currently in the back of a limo, on their way to the country church miles out of the city.

"I had no idea Ethan was so sentimental," Hannah said with a smile. "Choosing the church Jackson and I were married in is so sweet."

Allie couldn't stop smiling; she was almost giddy with emotion. There had never been a time in her life that she'd ever been this happy, this complete. Taking a chance, opening up to Ethan, had been the biggest risk she'd ever taken, and oh how he'd been the biggest reward. He had completely opened up to her, and they had both changed.

"Still. Don't you think it would have been cool to have a giant wedding in one of those places you see in the magazines? With, like, hundreds of people?"

Allie rolled her eyes. "Nope. Neither of us wanted that. We've invited the people that matter most to us. I couldn't ask for anything more," she said, glancing out the window. Snow was falling down hard, and the rolling countryside was blanketed in pristine white snow. They were running very late and she'd tried texting Ethan to let him know, but the message kept failing. She hoped he wasn't worried.

"You know how happy I am for you, right? Ethan is like a brother to me, and I always knew he'd come around and figure out what he needed."

Allie felt her eyes tear up as she smiled at her best friend. "Thank you," she whispered. "I never would have guessed, when we were on this road on our way to your wedding, that I was about to meet my future husband. Or that we'd all be here today."

"It was all meant to be," Hannah said, reaching across and squeezing her hand.

"I need to find myself one of these rich dudes like you two did," Dani said. "Who's left out of their group?"

"Just Nicholas Wright. Apparently their other friend Hayden is getting married in the spring. Never mind that anyway. You are *way* too young to even be considering any of their friends. Besides, I thought Max was the love of your life?"

Dani smirked. "Of course he is. I just can't let him know that or he'll get cocky."

"Daddy said Uncle Ethan is out of control," Emily said with a grin. Allie looked down and laughed as her goddaughter snuggled into her side.

"Ethan's been a bit nervous this week, I think," Hannah said, smiling.

Dani rolled her eyes. "Why? It's not like you're going to leave him at the altar or something."

"Ten bucks says Allie leaves Ethan at the altar."

Ethan would have given his best man, Jackson, the finger, had they not been standing at the front of the church. The guests were all seated, and soft music from the harpist was hopefully drowning out their conversation.

"I'm in. Maybe she decided she could do better."

Ethan shut his eyes and rolled back on his heels, ignoring his other stupid friend, Hayden. He and Allie should have just eloped on an island. Without friends.

"I'm in, too. Way too good for Ethan," Nicholas said.

Someone slapped him on the back and he opened his eyes, shooting them all dirty looks. "She's not leaving me at the altar. They're just late because of the weather."

"Everyone else made it okay," Nicholas said, pointing out the obvious.

Ethan swallowed hard. He had already thought of that. His gaze wandered the crowd, already knowing all the faces he would see. There was Max and Denise from the shelter. Hayden's fiancée, Alexandra McAllister, the Sampsons, and Annie. His eyes focused on her, and she gave him a wide smile. The noise from his friends' chatter continued and a rush of emotion swam through him, filling him with gratitude. For being here. For being alive, healthy. For Allie. God, so much gratitude for Allie.

The doors swung open and suddenly she was there, snow swirling around her, and for a second he couldn't breathe. Every single part of him was so filled to the brim with emotion he didn't know he was capable of. She was everything to him. And she was here. She was wearing a long, beaded ivory gown that fit her like a glove. The beads sparkled under the candlelight, her long hair shiny and loose around her shoulders. It was probably wrong to already be thinking about how he wanted to take the dress off her later, but hell, he was only human.

"Shit. Looks like we owe Ethan ten bucks," Jackson whispered.

Thankfully, his friends' stupid comments snapped him into the present, and he smiled at Allie. Jackson's kids made their way down the aisle first. The fact that Jackson had managed to have such cute kids was solely because of Hannah. Next came Hannah and Dani. Dani gave him a troublemaker wink before settling in beside Hannah and Jackson.

He blinked back the moisture in his eyes when everyone stood as Allie made her way down the aisle. But hell, he couldn't wait for her, so he met her halfway. He'd waited his entire life for Allie. He'd waited his entire life not to be alone. Alone, he could only be so much. With Allie, he was everything.

About the Author

Victoria James always knew she wanted to be a writer and in grade five, she penned her first story, bound it (with staples) and a cardboard cover and did all the illustrations herself. Luckily, this book will never see the light of day again.

In high school she fell in love with historical romance and then contemporary romance. After graduating University with an English Literature degree, Victoria pursued a degree in interior design and then opened her own business. After her first child, Victoria knew it was time to fulfill the dream of writing romantic fiction.

Victoria is a hopeless romantic who is living her dream, penning happily-ever-after's for her characters in between managing kids and the family business. Writing on a laptop in the middle of the country in a rambling old Victorian house would be ideal, but she's quite content living in suburbia with her husband, their two young children, and very bad cat.

Victoria would love to hear from her readers!
Visit her website: www.victoriajames.ca

Also by Victoria James...

FALLING FOR HER ENEMY

Alex McAllister always dreamed of a life filled with family, but being abandoned at a young age left her wary of letting anyone in. Now that she's settled in Still Harbor, Alex is faced with the magnetic pull of Hayden Brooks, the handsome workaholic who claims he's the biological father of her adopted daughter. A paternity test is all that's standing between Alex and her dream, but Hayden's about to make the most shocking decision of his life, just in time for Christmas...

THE RANCHER'S SECOND CHANCE

RESCUED BY THE RANCHER

A RISK WORTH TAKING

THE BEST MAN'S BABY

THE DOCTOR'S FAKE FIANCÉE

THE BILLIONAIRE'S CHRISTMAS BABY

FALLING FOR THE P.I.